HIS DEMANDS
AN AGE GAP, BILLIONAIRE BOSS ROMANCE

K.C. CROWNE

Copyright © 2024 by K.C. Crowne

All rights reserved.

No part of this book may be reproduced in any form or by any electronic or mechanical means, including information storage and retrieval systems, without written permission from the author, except for the use of brief quotations in a book review.

DESCRIPTION

**The silver fox billionaire is used to getting anything he wants...
And now, he wants to make me his darling little wife.**

Working as Ivan Stepanov's assistant is a literal gig from h*ll.
After a day of catering to his every demand I text my friend in haste:
'I HATE my boss but find him so freakin HOT!"

I arrive home with my thoughts stuck on the gorgeous older man ruining my life.
Moments later I'm in my tub lost in ecstasy, screaming Ivan's name.

KNOCK. KNOCK.

Dripping wet, I put on a robe and head to the front door.
It's Ivan with a rather ***large*** stiffness in his trousers.

"That text to your friend? You sent it to me."

Then he brings his face inches from mine. ***"Incase you're wondering, whatever you imagined in there doesn't come close to the real thing."***

My cheeks blush with embarrassment. ***"Will you show me?"***

That night was everything.
My first sweet taste of submission.
But nothing could have prepared me for Ivan's list of demands the next day...

"Move in with me. Marry me. Have my baby."

I stand up in shock, ***"I'll get back to you…"***

To which he responds: ***"This isn't up for discussion. You're not going anywhere."***

CHAPTER 1

JULIE

"I asked for this to be emailed, Miss Goodacre."

His eyebrow lifts.

That trademark, enigmatic expression of his that cuts straight to the core.

Ivan Stepanov's endless demands have finally tipped the scales.

Since the break of day, I've been twisting myself into knots to meet his needs, especially after dragging myself out of the office at 10:00 P.M. the previous evening.

I haven't had a moment's peace today, and now, without having had my lunch at 3:00 PM I'm just about ready to call it quits. Hangry is an understatement at this point.

"Oh, it's been sent," I retort, sprinkling just the right amount of sass into my words. "But given its vanishing act last time, I thought a hard copy might stick around longer."

The devil in an Armani suit looks at me, his gaze as penetrating as a laser.

He lifts his eyebrow again.

I'd bet a million dollars he popped out of the womb with that intimating expression.

Intimidating and sexy.

It's in fleeting moments like this I find myself admiring just how unforgivably handsome Ivan Stepanov is. Despite my best efforts.

It's unfair really.

His perfectly tailored suit, the smattering of gray in this stubble, those piercing eyes—nothing's out of place.

The tall, dark, and brooding thing really works for him. If only his personality matched the exterior.

Wishful thinking.

With the elegance of a maestro, Ivan navigates to his inbox, spots the email, and dives into a reply. All business, no pleasantries.

Then, without missing a beat, he's onto his next demand. "I'll be having a late lunch from that Mediterranean place on 5th. They're always swamped, just so you know. Please tend to the paperwork on your desk when you return."

Being an assistant to a man who thinks the world revolves around his wants requires a particular brand of insanity.

If I didn't need this job so badly, I might just have the courage to tell him where to shove his five star meal.

"Thank you, Miss Goodacre."

Clearly, my time's up.

As I make my way to Medina, the city's rhythm pulsates through the streets, a symphony of honking taxis, chattering pedestrians, and the ever-present tune of sirens in the distance.

Navigating Manhattan Financial District is akin to playing a real-life game of Tetris, where I dart and weave through an obstacle course of tourists mesmerized by skyscrapers stopping to snap a photo of literally everything.

It's a dance of waiting, smiling politely, and gently nudging the staff with a reminder that I am there to pick up an urgent business lunch for Stepanov Holdings to get the order expedited.

Upon securing the culinary treasure, I return to Stepanov Holdings Headquarters. The building, much like Ivan, stands tall, imposing, and unapologetically opulent.

By the time I return, holding Ivan's gourmet lunch and my modest salad, he's vanished.

Typical.

As I settle down to tackle the mountain of paperwork he's generously left behind, my desk phone starts ringing off the hook.

My phone becomes a hot potato, passing from one crisis to another with the skill of a seasoned diplomat promising that Mr. Stepanov will indeed return all calls, knowing fully well he won't.

Between bites of my salad and sips of coffee that's already gone cold, I navigate the treacherous waters of high finance by soothing egos and making promises I can only hope Ivan will keep.

I close my eyes and take a deep breath.

A smidgen of recognition from Ivan wouldn't hurt.

Some acknowledgment of the tireless effort behind making his life run as smoothly as a well-oiled machine.

As I glance at his untouched lunch, a part of me wants so badly to dump it on over his head. I'll have to save that vision for my next daydream.

Ivan sweeps back into the office like a stormfront.

"The paperwork, Miss Goodacre," he says, his voice cutting through the air like a knife.

My eyes dart between the semi-conquered paper mountain and him. "I didn't forget." I start, trying to keep the frustration from my voice. "Your clients have been calling nonstop, and I've been doing my best to keep them from losing their cool."

He fixes me with a look that could freeze lava. "Ten minutes."

I open my mouth to protest, but the look in his eyes stops me—the unyielding demand, the expectation of perfection.

In his world, there's no room for excuses, no space for the human element.

He leans in, his voice dropping to a harsh whisper. "I hired you because I thought you could handle the pressure. Don't prove me wrong."

With that parting shot, he strides away, leaving me feeling about two inches tall.

It's moments like these that I question my life choices.

Anger and frustration bubble up inside me like a shaken soda bottle, threatening to explode. But I refuse to cry, refuse to show any weakness in this high-stakes game of corporate chess.

Instead, I channel all that emotion into finishing the paperwork, my fingers flying over the keyboard like a pianist in the midst of a frenzied solo.

Feeling like I could blow up any minute.

Finally, with the printouts in hand, I march to Ivan's office.

I drop the papers onto his desk with a deliberate thump, watching them scatter forcefully.

He looks up, his expression unreadable as the papers flutter across his desk.

"That's everything you asked for," I announce, my voice quivering with a storm of suppressed fury. "Now if you don't mind, I'm clocking out for the rest of the day." The words hang between us, a bold line drawn after a day where every ounce of my patience was tested.

For a moment, Ivan only watches me, his dark eyes giving nothing away.

It's infuriating, like shouting into a void and waiting for an echo that never comes.

Ivan finally breaks the tense silence, his voice as steady and composed as ever, betraying no sign of irritation or amusement. "Miss Goodacre, you're free to leave," he says, his tone embodying the very essence of professional detachment he has practically made as his signature.

I quietly leave his office, my heart pounding like a drum in my chest.

I gather my things, pretending to be calm, my hands shaking as I shove my laptop into my bag.

I could totally be fired tomorrow. Fuck it.

I don't look back as I leave, the doors closing behind me with a finality that feels oddly satisfying.

The cool air hits my face, and I take a deep breath, trying to let go of the anger and the frustration.

As I walk, my mind keeps replaying the scene in Ivan's office.

That unreadable look in his eyes, was it indifference or something else?

CHAPTER 2

JULIE

Oh fuck. What have I done?

The moment I stepped outside Stepanov Holdings, the fiery anger starts to dissipate, replaced by a creeping sense of regret.

Do better Julie.

This job is supposed to be my golden ticket.

The paycheck is the stuff of daydreams, capable of turning visions into reality.

In just two more years of playing assistant, I could save enough to launch Goodacre Cares, the nonprofit I've been dreaming of since forever. Named in honor of my mother.

She didn't die in vain.

I'd make damn sure of that.

As I trudge through Manhattan's maze, I can't help but wonder if I've just torpedoed my dream.

What if Ivan decides I'm more trouble than I'm worth?

What if I get the dreaded pink slip?

After how I drew the line today there's no way I can assume otherwise.

New plan—march into the office tomorrow, head held high, and act like nothing happened. I'll do my job, exceed his expectations, and with any luck, Ivan will chalk up today's episode to a bad day and move on.

It's not like we haven't had our share of rough patches. He isn't the kind of boss you can have a heart-to-heart with over coffee. He's all about results, the bottom line.

Maybe he'll appreciate my drive, even if it did come out in a less-than-ideal manner.

As I navigate the city streets, my mind races with possibilities. Will he confront me? Will he pretend nothing happened? Or, worst of all, will he have security escort me out the moment I step through the door?

My aunt Barb would have a field day about this. She's one of the few people who knows the ins and outs of my job and my struggles with Ivan. I take my phone out of my purse and send her a text.

Today was the worst day ever!!!

I hate my boss!!

Why does he have to be so frickin' HOT???, my message says.

Just as I'm poised to flesh out my message with more details, the rumble of my approaching subway cuts through my thoughts, signaling an imminent loss of connection. I swiftly press Send and slide my phone back into my pocket, seamlessly melding with the flow of commuters as I step aboard.

Tomorrow, it's back to the grind. Julie Goodacre, the unflappable, the unstoppable. I'll tackle those spreadsheets, charm those clients, and keep Ivan's empire running without a hitch.

And who knows? Maybe this little blip will be the wake-up call we both needed.

Maybe it'll be the start of something new.

Either way, bring it on Ivan.

I'm ready for round two.

∼

Stomping into my apartment, I'm still simmering with a mix of anger and regret.

"Kiki?" I call out to my cat.

The living room window by the emergency fire escape is cracked open. I leave it for my cat to go out if she feels like it. She always comes back, my sweet grey furball. I'm guessing she's out exploring the neighborhood rooftops again.

My place, nestled in the Upper East Side, is a cozy, charming space—a splash of pastel colors amidst the concrete jungle, filled with soft throws, an overstuffed couch that's perfect for sinking into after a long day, and bookshelves crammed with everything from classic literature to self-help books that I swear I'll get around to reading someday.

Frustration gnawing at me, I head to the bathroom, deciding that if I can't drown my sorrows in a sea of apologies and understanding from Ivan, I'll do it in a warm bath.

After lighting some candles and filling my tub with warm water and lavender scented bubble bath I strip my clothes off and prepare for bliss.

As the hot water pours over me, I let out a sigh that feels like it's been building up for ages.

The tension in my muscles is gradually soothed, easing my mind. Soon enough, thoughts of Ivan return, only they're not the angry thoughts I typically have of him.

Those dark, brooding eyes, that gorgeous olive toned skin, that chiseled jawline that looks like it was carved by Michelangelo himself.

The vision of him persisting in my head like this does things to me.

Things that make my hands travel downward. My fingers slide between slick folds.

"Oh, wow," I groan softly, realizing how aroused I already am. I might as well do this. It'll take the edge off. Besides, I'm the mistress of my domain here.

My thoughts are mine and mine alone, no matter how wrong or dirty or decadent they may be.

I turn the water off and pat myself dry with a towel and head to my couch. Once I'm settled, I go back to where I left things off, feeling my clit swollen with unkempt desire.

As my fingers work their magic, my thoughts take an unexpected turn.

Fantasizing about Ivan should be off-limits, a line I don't cross. But as the warmth of my throw blanket blends with the rhythm of my fingers teasing my clit, the fantasy takes on a life of its own.

I close my eyes, letting my mind wander back to Ivan, his brooding gaze and chiseled features the perfect material for a harmless fantasy.

Ivan's stern face softens, his eyes revealing a depth I've never seen. His voice, usually sharp with demands, whispers kinky little secrets in my ears, and his touch, so often imagined as brusque, becomes tender and exploratory.

I let out a breath I didn't know I was holding, my body responding to the fantasy despite my brain's protests. It's like I'm on autopilot, caught up in a current too strong to fight against.

Ivan Stepanov, my horrible boss, the man who drives me up the wall, is now the star of my most intimate moment.

As my fingers continue their work of spectacular precision, I think that maybe there's more to my frustration than meets the eye. Could it be that beneath the layers of professional annoyance and irritation, there's a flicker of something else? Something more personal?

I shake my head, trying to clear it of such forbidden thoughts. But as I sink deeper into the sofa, the lines between reality and fantasy blur. For now, in the safety of my inner sanctuary, I'll let the fantasy run its course. Tomorrow, back in the real world, I'll deal with the consequences.

I imagine him rising from his desk, those coffee-dark eyes on mine. He strides over to me, undoing the Windsor knot of his tie. He knows what he wants, and just like anything else in this world, he's not afraid to take it.

He places his hands on my hips, squeezing my curves through the fabric of my skirt. Tingles rush through me, starting between my legs and spreading to every corner of my body. He leans in and kisses me, not giving a damn about propriety.

I resist a bit at first, wondering if giving myself over and letting him take me is right. But the longer I kiss him, the more his tongue probes my mouth, his musky taste filling me, the more I know it is.

I pull off his tie as he unfastens the buttons of my work blouse. The office air is cool against my skin, but his hands are soon all over my body, his touch surprisingly rough given his line of work. We continue to kiss, Ivan stripping me down until I'm in nothing but my work heels, bra, and panties.

With one more of his trademark glares, this one smoldering with sexual intensity, he wraps his arm around my waist and guides me over to the desk. He's just as commanding with intimate matters as he is with work.

Once I'm at the desk, he steps behind me, putting one hand on my upper back and bending me over. Back in the real world, I slip two fingers inside myself, burning with anticipation. What I wouldn't give to have him stretching me like this.

"Oh, yes!" I hiss as the orgasm blows through me, my pussy clenched and rippling delightedly. "IVAN, YES!" I cry out, moaning as I ride the wave and finger-fuck myself into sheer madness.

I say his name, over and over, as my body bucks and shudders.

It takes a while for me to come down from these clouds of my own making.

My cheeks burn.

I need some wine. This feeling, a mixture of guilt and awkwardness melting into the sweetest afterglow of a particularly intense orgasm—I've never experienced it before.

It's hard to get up. My thighs feel like jelly. I'm just about ready to stand on my own two feet again when the doorbell rings.

"What the..." I'm not expecting anybody. Nevertheless, the second ring has me jumping up and tiptoeing over to the door so I can peek through the peephole.

Holy shit!

Ivan is outside my door.

My heart skips a few beats. My blood freezes and boils at the same time, otherwise I can't explain this sudden light-headedness that's come over me.

Yet my hands react before my brain can stop it. I grab my robe, quickly put it on, then open the door, staring at Ivan in sheer disbelief.

"Um, hello?"

He stills at the sight of me.

My hair is a half-wet mess and my silk lace robe hugs my generous curves in all the right places.

There's also something wildly different about him.

The dark look in his eyes has me feeling he could eat me alive.

As I study him some more I notice a shamelessly generous bulge protruding from his pants.

Is that a boner?

It makes me lick my lower lip as my gaze travels back up to find him looking at me with that same darkness in his eyes.

Then he finally breaks the silence.

"You know that text you sent about you hating me?"

Dread grabs me by the throat and stiffens my joints as I understand what's happening. "I... I..." I can't say anything else.

"You sent that to me." He takes a deep breath and a step toward me.

Just like that, the distance between us shrinks.

The air thickens.

My lungs fail me.

I'm a deer caught in the headlights, and Ivan is about to destroy me. "In case you were wondering, whatever you imagined in here doesn't come close to how I can make you feel."

"What are you talking about?"

Ivan raises his eyebrow at me. Again, I don't know what to make of it. "I've been standing here for a while now, trying to figure out the best way to approach the issue of that text you sent me."

"It was a mistake," I mumble.

"What happened in here didn't sound like a mistake."

I glance over my shoulder. The sofa. Oh, boy, he heard me. He heard me calling out his name. This can't be happening!

He heard me pleasuring myself, imagining him in the most decadent way possible and crying out for him, mid-orgasm.

There's no unringing that bell.

And the bulging erection in his pants only serves to confirm that he's not here to berate me about a stupid text.

My core tightens. It's a slippery slope.

But it feels like the universe heard my wish and is granting me the opportunity to take it.

Say something Julie.

Anything.

"Will you show me?", my voice comes out in a whisper.

"Show you what?" He sounds horny as hell, but also angry.

That turns me on even more.

"How you can make me feel."

Our gazes lock.

I stop breathing altogether.

I can see him struggling, like he's doing everything in his power to hold back from letting his inner demons loose.

Finally he takes a deep breath, straightens his posture as he licks his lips.

Then he takes another step forward.

We're both inside my apartment now.

Slowly, the door closes behind him.

I lose track of time and space, abandoning my senses as I let his heated gaze swallow me whole.

"Take that off." His voice is heavy and surly.

I obey his command. My resistance is at an all-time low.

With trembling fingers, I peel the robe off my shoulders and let it land on the floor.

He takes his sweet time measuring me from head to toe, like his eyes are memorizing every curve in sight.

My cheeks flush with warmth.

And a shadow of a smile tests his lips.

"Turn around," he says.

Fuck. I'm putty in his hands.

I do as he says, holding my breath as he comes closer.

Closer, still.

I feel his breath burning into the back of my neck.

"What are you doing?" I foolishly ask, but my nipples perk up with excitement.

"You're done talking," he replies, and I almost whimper under his scorching authority.

He's the dominant type. I had no idea I wanted to be so submissive, but here I am aroused by his very words.

My heart's racing as I hear him open his pants.

Seconds later, he takes me in his arms, and I tremble like a leaf in his hands. He kisses the side of my neck, one hand grabbing my breast and squeezing it, tighter and tighter, while the other finds its way down to my clit, still tender from earlier.

"Oh..." I moan, tilting my head back. I inhale deeply, drunk on his cologne, while his fingers work my slick pussy into a whole new kind of frenzy.

My fantasy just became a reality, and I cannot stop whatever is about to happen.

Nor do I want to.

Ivan's breath is ragged as he pinches my nipple until it stings, his warm hardness against my slick pussy. I groan and squirm, yearning for him to be inside of me. But he's holding back, torturing me in only the way Ivan could.

"Tell me what you want," he says, his voice so low I can feel it in my bones.

"I want you." My voice so husky I can barely talk.

"Show me."

With that, I reach back and take hold of his huge cock, a soft moan escaping me as I wrap my fingers around him, savoring his thickness.

I place him at my entrance, his head spreading my lips. He exhales sharply and pulls back. "Oh, no, not yet," Ivan says. "I want you to bend over."

He doesn't tell me twice. He shows me, instead. Pressing one hand down my back, he pushes me into a bend, my legs spread before him. I can barely stand, but his fingers dig into my flesh as he spreads me open and gets down on his knees behind me.

His tongue reaches me first.

I'm done for.

He licks my pussy, tasting and probing, suckling my clit until I lose my senses altogether. I feel one hand letting go, fingers testing my entrance.

"You taste like fucking heaven, Julie. It's a dangerous weapon, what you've got here," Ivan growls, then proceeds to savagely finger-fuck me until I whimper in his hold. "Touch yourself for me."

"Ivan."

"Do it. Touch yourself like I just touched you."

He's got three fingers inside me and his other hand joins in on the action, thumb teasing my swollen nub while I cup my breasts and squeeze and pinch. My nipples sting, all the blood rushing out of my head as Ivan brings me closer and closer to that razor sharp edge.

"Come for me," he says.

It's like an automated instinct. I come for him. I come so hard, as he licks my pussy and feverishly rubs my clit, squeezing every last drop as I fall apart. "Oh God!" I gasp when he hoists me off the ground and carries me onto the sofa.

"I'm not done yet," he says.

I'm a rag doll. He can do whatever he wants with me. My body is still immobile in the aftermath of this devastating orgasm when he dives face first back between my legs.

"Ivan," I whisper, the name rolling off my tongue like a secret I've been keeping for too long.

"I like the way my name sounds on your lips" he says, then takes me in his mouth again.

The air thickens, charged with an electric current of forbidden desire. His strong hands trace the contours of my body, exploring every inch with a reverence that's both surprising and intensely arousing. His touch is a paradox—gentle yet commanding—never-ending waves of pleasure crashing over me.

"Ivan," I say again, louder this time. The walls of my apartment fade away, replaced by an intimate cocoon where only he and I exist. His presence is overwhelming, consuming, guiding me toward a crescendo of ecstasy.

As yet another climax builds, my body tenses, every nerve ending singing with anticipation. "Ivan," I cry out, the name a talisman that unleashes the final wave of pleasure. It crashes over me, a tsunami of sensation that leaves me breathless and spent.

He shoves three fingers inside me, a deep, animal grunt escaping his lips as he watches me unravel, the pleasure gripping me like a fist. "Fucking hell," he whispers, unable to take his eyes off me as I writhe in the purest form of existence.

I don't how long it takes for me to see again. But by the time I register the movement, Ivan is already zipping his pants back up and headed for the door.

"I'll see you tomorrow."

It's all he says, and I've got nothing. Only my jumbled thoughts.

He might be insufferable, but in the realm of fantasy, he was fair game. I didn't think anything would ever happen between us in the real world. But it did.

He's off-limits, a line I can't cross. But I crossed it.

I might just sink into this couch and die. The embarrassment, the horror, the absolute mortification of it all! What the hell is going to happen tomorrow? How in God's green earth am I going to walk into the office in the morning?

For a wild second I consider fleeing the country, changing my name, maybe joining a remote convent where phones are banned. But that's the panic talking. I'm Julie Goodacre, not some damsel in distress who runs at the first sign of trouble.

CHAPTER 3

IVAN

The soft glow of the city lights casts a warm hue through the windows of my Upper West Side brownstone. As I bask in the midnight moonlight, I decide to numb my mind.

Favoring the quiet night ahead, I head to my home bar—a custom-built piece in rich mahogany—and start fixing myself a drink. The clink of ice against glass is a familiar, soothing sound, a moment of calm in the relentless pace of my world.

As I pour the whiskey, its amber shade reflecting the city's glow, my thoughts drift back to Julie's outburst earlier today.

She had acted like a petulant child, and my first instinct was not to reward such behavior with my attention. I didn't think I'd have time for such theatrical displays of emotion; I need efficiency, competence, and control—the same principles that guide my business decisions. But then she sent me that text by mistake, and all hell broke loose inside of me.

As the smooth whiskey warms me, I can't help but reflect on the situation with a touch of sardonic amusement. I showed her, didn't I? And she sure as hell showed me. Going to her apartment was a mistake I will probably regret for the rest of my life, but I enjoyed it too much. The sound of her voice calling out my name as she comes... it's fucking priceless. Perhaps I was too harsh, a bit of an asshole even.

Julie is more than competent. She's a damn good assistant, the kind who anticipates problems before they arise and handles them with a finesse that often goes unnoticed. And the way her body quivers, the way her pussy clenches around me...

Losing her over a moment of irritation would be a poor business decision, and I don't make those. The thought of having to train someone new, to deal with the inevitable incompetence that comes with inexperience, is almost as distasteful as acknowledging that I might have been in the wrong.

I take a sip of my drink, letting the rich, oaky flavors linger on my tongue. The truth is, Julie's outburst, while unprofessional, was not entirely unjustified. I push my people hard, and I expect the best because I give the best. But even I can admit, albeit grudgingly, that my approach can be abrasive.

The realization doesn't sit comfortably with me. I've built my empire on being tough, on not yielding an inch unless it benefits me. Showing leniency and understanding are not qualities I'm known for.

Yet as I stand in the quiet of my home, I can't shake the feeling that maybe, just once, I should consider a different approach. The genie is out of the bottle, anyway. We did something I never do with the people I employ. That kind of intimacy cannot be wiped away with a sponge. It can't be wiped away with anything. I want more of it. So much more. I need to be inside her, to feel her wet softness wrapped around my cock. I need to hear my name rolling off her tongue again.

If I'm to be brutally honest with myself, Julie's earlier behavior caught me off guard. In the time she's worked for me, she's always been the epitome of calmness, of stoic composure. Today, she broke. Tonight, I may have broken her further.

She reveals very little of herself, her emotions carefully guarded behind a professional facade. It's a trait I've come to respect, and yet her display of unbridled passion today was unsettling.

There's no denying that she's an exceptionally attractive woman. From the moment I hired her, I've been acutely aware of her appealing presence.

She possesses a kind of understated beauty that doesn't scream for attention but instead whispers for it, compelling and serene. Her light blonde hair, a pale honey color, contrasts strikingly with the depth and clarity of her blue eyes, eyes that seem to hold secrets and stories I've yet to uncover.

And her body, it's as if it's been sculpted to perfection. She's petite, yet her curves are pronounced, giving her a silhouette that's both delicate and alluring. My fingers still tingle, the memory of her breasts imprinted on my skin.

She moves in a graceful, almost ballet-like manner, each gesture controlled and precise. Her preference for pastels in stylish, form-fitting attire only accentuates her figure, highlighting her femininity in a way that's both subtle and undeniable.

As her boss, I've always maintained a professional distance, keeping my personal thoughts and feelings well in check. But I'd be lying if I said I haven't caught myself lingering on her form more than once, appreciating the visual pleasure she provides. Well, I caught myself doing a lot on top of that, tonight. Damn.

It's not just her physical appearance, either. It's the whole package with the way she carries herself, her intelligence, her efficiency. She's about the sexiest woman I've ever laid eyes on, and today's entire dynamic revealed a fiery passion that I find unexpectedly arousing.

My name echoes in the sound of her voice. Arousal hits me with an intensity that's as unexpected as it is powerful, and I'm instantly hard.

My stomach tightens as a familiar heat courses through me, pooling in my lower abdomen. It's a primal, uncontrollable response. I continue to remember, transfixed, the realization of what I'm doing to myself only amplifies my desire.

Ivan. The way she said it, breathy, laden with desire, it was like a punch to the gut, a direct line to every carnal instinct I possess. Hearing her say my name in such a context—so intimate and raw—nearly caused my undoing. I had no choice, standing outside her door. It was a sign. It was a revelation, a crossing of a line I didn't even realize was there to be crossed.

I'm torn between shock and a deep, burning arousal. Part of me wants to stop this, to politely pull the plug tomorrow and end everything right then and there. But another part of me—one I usually keep under strict control—urges me to keep pursuing this, to indulge in this unexpected and intensely erotic experience. To find and break her every limit.

My grip on my cock tightens, my knuckles turning white. The rational part of my mind is losing ground quickly to the irrational part. The sound of Julie experiencing such uninhibited pleasure, and the knowledge that she thinks of me during it, is intoxicating, even now, long after I've already tasted her.

As Julie's moans fill the space of my mind, over and over again, my imagination takes charge, painting vivid images behind my eyes. I picture her beneath me as I pump into her, one hand absentmindedly playing with a perky nipple, enhancing her pleasure.

I close my eyes, allowing the scene to unfold in my mind's eye. Julie, always so composed and efficient, is transformed in this fantasy, meant to pick up where we left off at her apartment. Here she is unguarded, sensual, and utterly captivating.

Throwing back the last of my whiskey, its warmth spreading through me like liquid fire, I find myself propelled through a tension that demands release.

It's a rare feeling, this loss of control, this overwhelming need coursing through me. But as I think of Julie, the sounds she made, her voice whispering my name in the throes of passion, a deep, primal response overtakes me with a fervor that brooks no argument.

"Fuck it," I mutter to myself, my decision made. I stroke myself tighter. The contact sends a jolt of pleasure through me, erasing any lingering doubts. With a swift, almost desperate movement, I let loose, replaying the very moment she came all over my face.

With a low groan I give in, allowing the memory of her to carry me through to a climax that's as intense as it is cathartic.

Afterward, as a semblance of my control returns, I find my thoughts drifting back to the reality of the situation. The message, the undeniable attraction, the lines that have been suddenly and irrevocably crushed, all coalesce into a decision that feels as inevitable as it is risky.

I pick up my phone, my fingers steady as I create a calendar invite for Julie. A meeting set for eight-fifteen tomorrow morning.

We have things to discuss, indeed.

As I send the invite, I can't help but feel a surge of anticipation. Tomorrow's meeting will be unlike any other. It's a step into uncharted territory, a venture into a dynamic that's as thrilling as it is uncertain.

CHAPTER 4

JULIE

Tossing my phone onto the kitchen charger like it's a hot potato, I make a beeline for my bed. The whole text message debacle has left me in a state of mental chaos, with embarrassment and anxiety duking it out for top billing. Then there's this constantly returning grin as I remember how Ivan squeezed every last drop of my climax with those soft, beautiful lips of his. Holy hell.

As I lay there in the dark, I start the process of convincing myself that everything will be fine. "Ivan's too busy to take this whole thing seriously," I mutter to the ceiling, an assumption meant to soothe my frayed nerves.

The more I think about it, the more it's probable. The man barely has time to breathe between meetings, let alone overthink everything we just did. Besides, he needs me. I am stellar at my job. He can't deny it.

I'm the gatekeeper to his world of high finance and endless negotiations.

Comforted by this logic, I almost convince myself. Almost. But then, sleep brings with it a dream that's too vivid, too accurate.

I toss and turn, caught in the throes of a fantasy that rapidly spiraled out of control.

So there I am, lying in bed, a bundle of nerves and hormones, fantasizing about my boss filling me to the brim, continuing what we started tonight while simultaneously dreading the very real possibility of professional suicide. It's as if my brain can't decide whether it's horny or horrified, so it settled on a maddening mix of both.

As the night drags on, sleep remains elusive. Every time I close my eyes I'm back in that same dream, with Ivan and my damn phone. And every time I wake up, it's with a sinking feeling that tomorrow is going to be one hell of a day at the office. Maybe my last.

I reluctantly drag myself out of bed, exhausted from the restless night of unwelcome dreams and thoughts, and too much tossing and turning. My phone feels like a ticking time bomb as I gingerly pick it up the next morning.

The screen lights up, a calendar invite from Ivan staring me in the face. It's a meeting request. Well, shit.

My heart plummets into my stomach and a cold sweat breaks out across my skin.

For a fleeting second, I entertain the idea of calling in sick. It would be so easy to hide away, to avoid facing the consequences of my actions. But that's not who I am. I don't run away from my mistakes. If Ivan is going to fire me for this, then so be it. I'll face it head-on. He partook in it, too. He carries some of the responsibility. I doubt I'll have the actual courage to say that to his face.

I stand in front of my wardrobe, my mind racing. This could be my last day at Stepanov Holdings, my final moments as Ivan's assistant. If that's the case, I'm going out in style.

As I head out the door, my mind replays the events of last night, over and over. It's like a bad yet dangerously catchy song stuck on repeat, each replay a fresh wave of embarrassment. But I square my shoulders, determined to face whatever comes.

The train ride to work is a blur, my mind a whirlwind of what-ifs and maybes. But one thing is clear—I'm going to walk into that office, head held high, and take whatever Ivan throws at me. In Armani and Louboutin's, no less.

The familiar hush of the building in the early morning feels different as I walk in, charged with an unspoken tension as I make my way to the nearly deserted floor. It's a quiet that usually brings a sense of peace, a moment to gather my thoughts before the whirlwind of the day. But today, it feels like the calm before a storm.

As always, I arrive just before seven forty-five, a routine that's become second nature. The floor is still, the only sounds present being the soft hum of the air conditioning and my own steady breathing. Ivan's already in his office. He's a man who thrives on being the first to arrive and the last to leave, his work ethic as relentless as it is impressive.

Dropping my stuff off at my desk, I take a moment to steady myself. My heart is racing, a fluttering bird trapped in a cage, as I mentally prepare for the impending meeting. This isn't just any regular morning briefing or review session.

This is a moment that could redefine everything.

With a deep breath that does little to calm my racing heart, I walk toward Ivan's office. Each step feels heavier than the last, my heels clicking against the floor like a metronome counting down to an inevitable conclusion. My mind is a whirlwind of thoughts and scenarios, each more nerve-wracking than the last.

I reach his door and pause. It's seven fifty-nine, sixteen minutes before the scheduled meeting time.

Part of me wants to just get this over with and march right into his office now, but I know how much he values a scheduled routine. So instead, I sit at my desk and turn on my computer, knowing there is no possible way I'm going to be able to concentrate on anything.

The minutes tick by in agonizingly slow fashion before finally the reminder on my phone goes off.

Eight-fifteen.

The moment of truth has arrived.

CHAPTER 5

JULIE

"Come in, Miss Goodacre."

His voice, low and quiet, filters through the door, sending a shiver down my spine. The way he said my name felt different, a tone I haven't heard before. It's enough to heighten the tension that's been building since I stepped off the elevator.

Taking a deep breath, I push the door open and step inside, closing it softly behind me. The familiar surroundings of Ivan's office offer no comfort today; instead, they feel like the setting of an interrogation room, every item a potential witness to my impending professional doom.

His back is to me, he's focused on his computer screen. I take the few steps to stand before his desk, feeling like a defendant awaiting a verdict.

The silence stretches, filled only with the soft clicks of his keyboard. The waiting is agonizing, it's like standing on the edge of a cliff, unsure whether I'll be pushed or pulled back to safety.

Finally, unable to bear the silence any longer, I part my lips to speak. But he beats me to it before a single word can escape.

"Thank you for your promptness." His tone is calm, almost amused, and I get the distinct impression he's enjoying this, feeling me squirm under the weight of my own embarrassment.

When he finally swivels around to face me, I muster the courage to meet his gaze, and it's like looking into the eye of a storm—dark, deep, and tumultuous.

He looks at me, his eyes searching, probing. The intensity of his stare is unnerving, and I feel the heat rising in my cheeks, a telltale sign of discomfort. There's something in his gaze that's both unsettling and compelling, a depth I've never seen before.

My voice, when it finally shows up, is a mixture of defiance and vulnerability. "Mr. Stepanov, I..."

I can't seem to find the right words. The tension between us, the unspoken source of it, feels like it's eating me up whole. It's a standoff, a silent battle of wills, and for the first time, I'm unsure of my footing.

The familiar dynamics of boss and assistant have shifted, leaving us in uncharted territory.

Apology hanging in the air between us, I clamp my lips shut, resisting the urge to fill the silence with babbling explanations and excuses.

My mind is a whirlwind of thoughts, scenarios playing out in rapid succession, each more mortifying than the last. But outwardly I stand my ground, a statue of composure.

Finally, he mercifully breaks the silence, his voice cutting through the heavy air in the room.

"Do you find me attractive?" The question is so unexpected, so surprising, that it takes a moment for it to fully register. My heart stutters as my brain fumbles for a response. This isn't the conversation I anticipated, not by a long shot.

I stammer, a garbled mess of syllables that makes no sense. I stop, clear my throat, and force myself to start again.

"You are a handsome man," I admit, because denying it would be like denying the sky is blue. "But that's no excuse for what I've done." The words feel inadequate, a weak explanation for something that's far too complicated. For what *we've* done. That might've sounded fairer, but I'm the one who started this. I'm the one who set the fire, and boy, he only made it burn brighter.

The admission leaves me feeling exposed, like I've given him more ammunition, revealed another chink in my armor. But there's truth in it, an acknowledgment of the physical attraction that I've tried so hard to ignore, to bury under layers of professionalism and propriety.

My honesty hangs between us, a new variable in the complex equation of our relationship.

Ivan looks at me with a gaze that feels like it's trying to peer straight into my soul. "Tell me, Julie," he begins, his voice deceptively calm, using my first name in a way that feels entirely too intimate. "Was last night the first time you thought of me?"

I steady myself, meeting his probing eyes with a resolve I don't feel. "Yes," I reply, my voice as even as I can manage. "It was the first time."

Ivan's eyes narrow slightly, a hint of skepticism in his expression. "You expect me to believe that?" he asks.

His accusation of being deceptive slices through the air, sharp and unexpected. I stay silent, my brain racing. Where is this conversation going? Is this some sort of test, a game to gauge my honesty?

I clench my jaw, fighting the instinct to defend myself further. I choose silence instead, a refusal to engage in his game.

I begin to realize this is about more than just a text message; it's about maintaining control over my personal life, over the parts of me that aren't up for scrutiny or discussion.

The room seems to shrink when he stands. Ivan is an imposing figure, his presence overwhelming in the confines of his office. He moves around his desk, and as he towers over me, a rush of arousal hits me, unexpected and unwelcome. I fight to tamp it down, to maintain my composure under his scrutiny.

I don't step back as he approaches. Instead, I turn to face him, meeting his gaze head-on. I refuse to be intimidated, to show any weakness. But the proximity, the sheer physicality of him, is disconcerting.

I'm acutely aware of every inch of him, the power and strength that emanates from his frame. My mind can't help but to wander, remembering what it was like to be enveloped in those arms, to be the focus of all that intensity.

It's a thought I quickly squash, but not before it sends a thrill through me.

I brace myself for the words I'm sure are coming next, *you're fired*. It would be the logical conclusion to this bizarre meeting.

But what comes out of his mouth instead is so far from what I expected, it leaves me reeling.

"What do you think about marriage?"

CHAPTER 6

IVAN

"I'm sorry, did you say *marriage?*"

As I observe Julie's reactions, I can't help but feel a mix of admiration and intrigue. The purpose of this meeting was to apply pressure, to see how she'd react under the kind of stress that most people would break under. But she's holding her own, maintaining a composure that's both frustrating and fascinating.

There's a hint of embarrassment in her demeanor, a natural response given the circumstances. But it's her resilience, her ability to stand firm in the face of extreme discomfort, that truly catches my attention. It's a rare quality I admire.

Eventually, though, I see a flicker of confusion cross her face, a slight uncertainty in how to proceed. Good. Being off balance and unsure is exactly where I want her. It's these types of moments, these cracks in the facade, when true character is revealed.

When she stammers, it's a humanizing moment, one that should irritate me but instead strikes me as endearing. It's a glimpse of the person behind the professional mask, a hint of vulnerability that's unexpectedly appealing.

Julie pauses, clearly trying to gather her thoughts, and I watch her with a keen interest. She's more than just an assistant; she's a puzzle, a challenge, an enigma.

"I haven't really thought about marriage," she finally says, her voice steadier.

I've always prided myself on being able to read people, to anticipate their reactions and maneuver them accordingly. But Julie, she's different. She defies the patterns, the predictable responses.

"No boyfriend?" I press on, watching as her cheeks redden once more. The blush that spreads across her face is outrageously sexy and appealing, adding a layer of sensitivity to her otherwise composed exterior.

"I'm single," she answers immediately. There's an edge to her voice, a steeliness that speaks of more than just her relationship status. "I've been single for a while."

I decide to delve deeper, curious to see how far I can push her.

"What do you think of marriage?" I ask again, maintaining my composure.

Julie answers my question with silence. Her eyes, usually so expressive and vibrant, now hold a guarded wariness. I can almost see the wheels turning in her mind, trying to decipher the meaning behind my words, the intent of this unusual line of questioning.

Her frustration finds voice in a question laced with sarcasm and genuine inquiry. "Are you just making sure I won't be homeless if you fire me? Checking to see if I have a husband or boyfriend to fall back on?" Her words are sharp, her tone biting.

I can't help but chuckle, not out of amusement but at the absurdity of the idea. "No, Julie," I respond, my voice calm and assured. "I know you can take care of yourself." It's the truth. I've always admired her independence, her capability. Two qualities out of many that sets her apart.

"So what the hell are you doing then?" she demands, her voice tinged with both anger and confusion.

The raw emotion in her voice and the intensity of her gaze are a stark contrast to the usual composed assistant I'm used to. It's refreshing, and it solidifies the decision I've been contemplating.

The time has come to end her frustration, to lay my cards on the table. I look at her directly, making sure she understands the gravity of my words.

"I want a wife and child," I state plainly, holding her gaze to ensure she grasps the full meaning of my statement, that she knows how serious I am. The room feels charged with the weight of my confession, the air thick with implications and unspoken questions.

"And I think you're perfect for that job."

CHAPTER 7

JULIE

My mouth drops open in disbelief. "You can't be serious," I blurt out, convinced this must be some kind of twisted joke.

I've worked for the man for over a year; I know when he's playing and when he's dead serious. And right now, he's as serious as I've ever seen him.

As my mind races with all kinds of thoughts, I notice a subtle shift in Ivan's demeanor. His impeccable posture, always so controlled and commanding, appears even more pronounced, as if steeling himself for my reaction.

His eyes, often guarded and unreadable, hold a flicker of either anticipation or a challenge. It's hard to tell, but it's a departure from his typical stoic and confident expression.

He reaffirms his statement with unwavering certainty. "I'm very serious."

The resolve in his voice is unmistakable, and it sends a shiver down my spine. As he speaks, his jaw tightens ever so slightly, a physical manifestation of the determination in his words. It's a small movement, but in the quiet of his office, it feels significant.

I stare into his eyes, searching for any hint of jest, any small sign that this is all just a bizarre prank. But there's no hint of humor, no trace of a smirk. Just the steady gaze of a man who's used to getting what he wants.

Oddly, the intense determination to have me as his wife, his refusal to even entertain a 'no' makes him the sexiest damn man on the planet.

A part of me I didn't even know existed almost whispers a 'yes.' But then the absurdity of the situation crashes back into me. This isn't a fairy tale, it's my life, and his proposal is nothing short of insane.

An uncontrollable laughter bubbles up from somewhere deep inside, brought on by the irrationality and silliness of it all. It starts as a chuckle, then grows into full-blown, hysterical laughter. Tears start to stream down my face, my sides ache, and I can barely catch my breath.

Ivan just watches me, an unreadable expression on his face. He doesn't say a word, doesn't try to stop me. He just lets me laugh, his eyes following every movement, every shake of my shoulders.

It takes a good minute or two for me to get a handle on myself. I wipe the tears from my eyes, still chuckling softly.

"I'm sorry," I manage to say between residual giggles. "It's just... this is so unexpected."

He continues to watch me, and I wonder what he's thinking. Is he regretting his proposal, considering rescinding it? Or is he just recalculating his approach, like he does with every other challenge he faces?

His composure doesn't waver, not even for a second, as I pull myself away from the edge of hysteria. He's as cool and collected as ever, watching me with a curiosity that's both intimidating and strangely alluring.

I regain a bit of my composure. It's time to put him in his place. "I don't know what you're used to in Russia, but here in America, women don't ask how high when a man tells them to jump," I say, my tone laced with a mix of humor and defiance.

He responds smoothly, "I haven't lived in Russia for decades." His correction catches me off guard.

"Why do you think I would agree to a loveless marriage just so you can have a child?" I ask, my voice steadier now though my mind is racing with the implications of what he's proposing.

What he does next is completely unexpected. He steps closer, entering my personal space with a confidence that's as startling as it is unsettling. My stomach does a flip, and I feel my heart rate accelerate. Given what happened last night, I shouldn't be so startled by this move, but Ivan manages to make my chest tighten every time he comes near me.

The laughter that filled the room moments ago has vanished, replaced by an intense awkwardness. Ivan is close now, so close I can feel the warmth radiating from his body, sense the formidable presence that makes him who he is. It's overwhelming, the proximity, and a part of me wishes I could feel more than just his radiating warmth.

He speaks again, his voice low and assured. "Because I will take care of all your needs." The words hang in the air, and I'm acutely aware of the double entendre. It sends a jolt of awareness through me, and I'm suddenly very conscious of how close he is, of the implications of his words.

My mind is a whirlwind of thoughts, fantasies and the sudden, undeniable realization that my body is still reacting to him in a way it has no business doing. Honestly, I'd hoped that last night's episode might've taken the edge off. That I got over my desire for him. But I feel a heat spreading through me, a flush of arousal that's both embarrassing and exhilarating. There's no doubt in my mind that I'm going to need to change my panties after this meeting.

My boss, the man who just proposed a bizarre, business-like marriage, is standing in front of me, and all I can think about is how much I want him. How much I want to feel his hands on me, his lips against mine. How badly I need him inside me.

His next words snap me out of the daze his proximity had plunged me into.

"I know about your dream," he says, and my arousal is replaced by surprise. "The nonprofit," he continues, "named for your mother." His voice is matter-of-fact, but the content of his words sends a jolt through me.

I stare at him, my confusion clear. "How do you know about that?" The question comes out sharper than I intend, but the revelation that he's privy to my personal aspirations is unsettling.

"I've read your blog," Ivan admits, and the shock that ripples through me must be evident on my face. The idea that the man who seems to have little time for anything not directly related to his business has read my personal blog is almost too strange to believe.

He explains further, "I found it moving." He's never mentioned it before, never hinted that he knew about this side of me.

His next proposition, however, brings me back to the surreal reality of our conversation. "If you help me," he says, "I'll help you. I need an heir, and you need start-up funds. I want you to be my wife and have at least one child with me."

I feel my eyes widen in disbelief at his words. "You really are serious."

"Yes," he continues, undeterred by my reaction. "In exchange, I will provide the necessary funds to kickstart your nonprofit, the one you've dreamed of creating in memory of your mother."

It's a lot of unanticipated information to process. I can't deny the offer is tempting—a chance to start my nonprofit, to honor my mother's memory, is something I've been working toward for years. But marriage? A child? With Ivan?

The practicality of his offer is overshadowed by the enormity of its personal consequences. Marriage isn't a business deal; it's a commitment, a union, a partnership. And a child is a whole other life, a person who would depend on us, on me.

"I..." My voice trails off as I try to gather my thoughts. "This is a lot to take in, Ivan. You're talking about marriage, a child. This isn't just some business transaction I can make a quick decision on."

He looks at me with an uncharacteristic softness. "It's a practical solution to both our needs," he responds, his tone steady.

Practical. There's that word again. It's so typical of the man who views the world through a lens of efficiency and logic. But life, love, family—those aren't just practical matters. They're emotional, personal, complex.

The magnitude of Ivan's proposal leaves me grasping for words. "Would you expect me to continue working as your assistant?" I finally manage to ask, my voice tinged with incredulity.

His response is immediate yet thoughtful. "That will be your choice," he says. "But I would prefer if you stayed home with our child once he or she is born. From there, you could easily work on your nonprofit."

I'm speechless, my mind a blank canvas. The scenario he's painting of me being at home, raising our child, working on my dream project—it all feels like something out of a parallel universe. The theme to "The Twilight Zone" starts going off in my head.

It's tempting, undeniably so, but it's also a complete upheaval of everything I know. And he's not even done yet.

"I'll have a prenup drawn up by my lawyers," he continues, his voice calm. "You can read it at your leisure."

A prenup. Of course there'd be a prenup. Everything neatly arranged, legally binding, no loose ends. It's so like him to think of every detail, to plan for every eventuality.

"Any requests?" he asks.

The question catches me off guard. Requests? What kind of requests do you make in a situation like this?

I stare at him, trying to process everything he's just said. This isn't just a marriage proposal; it's a life-altering decision, a crossroads that could lead me down a path I'd never imagined.

"Requests?" I echo, my voice barely above a whisper. "I... I don't even know where to start." The truth is, I'm overwhelmed, trying to navigate this strange new territory between personal desires and professional boundaries.

Ivan watches me, waiting patiently for my response. But what can I say? What can I ask for in a situation as bizarre and unprecedented as this?

Seated there in his office, with the man I've known only as my boss offering me a future so radically different from anything I've ever considered, I realize the gravity of what's being asked of me.

This goes beyond any job offer or request. This is a complete transformation of my life as I know it.

CHAPTER 8

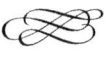

JULIE

"We can start with making one thing clear: you will be my wife, not my employee."

"What about *love*?"

He's unflappable, the word not giving him even a moment of pause. "If I were marrying for love, there would be a contract drawn up for that woman as well." He says it like it's the most obvious thing in the world, like love and contracts go hand in hand.

"So are you saying feelings aren't important to you?" I can't help but ask. It slips out, a genuine question amidst the absurdity of this whole situation.

"I want an heir," he says matter-of-factly, as if discussing a business merger rather than a child. "I didn't build this company to watch it die with me."

"You're worried about an heir? But why? I mean, I get why, but why *now*? You're still young; you've got all the time in the world. Not like you're a year away from retirement or something."

He responds with a small, almost imperceptible shrug, a hint of amusement in his eyes. "I'm forty-five. Not exactly old, but I don't have all the time in the world as you've stated."

"Oh, I didn't realize," I say, genuinely surprised by his age. I assumed he was in his mid- to late thirties, forty at most.

He looks at me, his gaze assessing. "Does the age difference bother you?" he asks, his voice neutral, giving nothing away.

"No, age isn't the problem. The problem is the ridiculousness of this whole situation."

To my surprise, Ivan reaches out and takes my hand, his touch firm yet not overbearing. He guides me to the sofa in the corner of his office, a piece of furniture that's always seemed more for show than actual use. We sit down, facing each other, and the unexpected intimacy is disarming. I'm close enough to see the subtle flecks of color in his dark eyes, the faint lines that speak of long hours and hard work.

Sitting on the couch so close to him, I feel like I'm on the verge of combusting. His touch, though simple and seemingly innocuous, feels intensely intimate. It's different from last night.

"I understand your hesitancy," he says, his voice low and soothing. His eyes hold mine, and I'm trapped in their depths, unable to look away. "But being my wife will open many doors for you."

I listen, half-dazed, as he outlines the benefits of the arrangement. "Your nonprofit will be a success from the start with the connections I can provide. And beyond that, you'll never have to worry about finances."

It's too much to try and process all at once. The practical side of me that's always planning and preparing, can see the logic in his words. The connections, the financial security, they're things I've dreamed of for my nonprofit, for the legacy I want to build in my mother's memory.

But then he adds something that sends a jolt through me. "If you wish to divorce after our child is grown, I'll ensure that you're well taken care of." The words hang in the air like an unwanted promise, a future so different from anything I've ever envisioned for myself.

Divorce. The word echoes in my mind. He's planning not only for our marriage and our child, but for the potential end of it all. It's so like him to think ten steps ahead, to plan for every contingency.

I'm torn between admiration for his foresight and a pang of sadness at the clinical nature of it all. Marriage, in my mind, has always been about love, about finding someone to share my life with, not a strategic partnership with exit strategies.

Sitting there with his hand still holding mine, I feel a swirl of emotions. Excitement, fear, confusion, and a strange sense of intrigue. My enigmatic boss is offering me a life that's both a dream and a challenge.

The practicalities, the benefits, they're alluring. But the personal cost, the emotional investment, that's a price I'm not sure I'm ready to pay. And yet as I sit with him, feeling the heat from his hand, listening to his well-reasoned proposal, I can't help but wonder *what if?*

A realization hits me like a cold wave, washing away the warmth that his touch had brought. He's not just asking for my hand in marriage; he's asking for decades of my life. The intimacy of the moment, the connection I thought I felt, all evaporate under the harsh light of this understanding.

He sees this, us, me, as nothing more than a transaction, a means to an end. The romantic, the dreamer in me, recoils at the thought. I can't just switch off my feelings and compartmentalize my life into neat, emotionless boxes like he does.

I'm a human, not a chess piece in his strategic game of life.

Gently, but with a firm resolve, I withdraw my hand from his. I need space, time to think and to process this proposition that's anything but romantic.

I open my mouth, ready to tell him that I'm taking the day off, that I need time to consider his offer and what it means for my future. But before the words can leave my lips, there's a knock on the office door.

CHAPTER 9

IVAN

A sudden knock at my office door gives me a jolt, shattering the delicate conversation with Julie. Such interruptions are unheard of in my rigorously controlled schedule, each minute accounted for, each meeting meticulously planned.

A sense of foreboding washes over me as I rise, offering Julie a brief, terse nod, an unspoken signal that something unexpected is afoot.

My heart rate quickens as I stride toward the door, a surge of adrenaline coursing through my veins. In my world, surprises are rarely pleasant, often harbingers of trouble. As I reach out and grasp the cool metal of the doorknob, a knot forms in the pit of my stomach, a primal instinct warning me of danger lurking on the other side.

I pull the door open, and my worst fears materialize before my eyes. Standing in the doorway, exuding a dangerous aura, are figures ripped straight from a chapter of my life I thought I had closed for good.

Two Russian gangsters with cold, calculating eyes, subtle bulges of concealed weapons beneath their shirts, are a clear threat, a reminder of a world I left behind.

And standing between them looms a ghost from my past. None other than Boris Abramov, the head of the Bratva I once served.

However, Boris has changed. The strong, intimidating figure I remember now replaced by a man who's let himself go. His once lean frame is now bulky, his suit straining against the added weight. His face, previously sharp and cunning, is now flushed with signs of overindulgence.

But his eyes, cold and calculating, haven't changed. They still hold a hint of the man who once commanded fear and respect in the circles we ran in.

The air around the men feels charged, the atmosphere heavy with the unspoken threats they bring.

"Greetings, Ivan," Boris says, his voice heavy with an accent that takes me back to my homeland. His eyes scan the room behind me, taking in the details with a predator's interest.

I stand in the doorway, a barrier between them and my world, a world that includes Julie, sitting just a few feet away. My mind races, calculating the potential reasons for this unexpected visit, the implications it carries, none of them good.

"Hello, Boris," I reply, my tone controlled, giving nothing away. "To what do I owe the pleasure of this visit?" My words are carefully chosen, a blend of caution and veiled hostility. The Bratva is not an entity one trifles with, and

Boris' presence here is a clear indication that the past is not as buried as I'd hoped.

He smirks, a hint of the cunning man I remember so well flickering in his eyes. "Oh, Ivan, can't an old friend stop by to catch up?" His words are light, but they carry a weight, a hidden meaning that's not lost on me. "You remember Sergei?"

Oh, I remember him alright. "Let's talk outside," I say, nodding down the hallway. "There's a conference room where we can—"

Boris, still an imposing figure despite his deteriorated state, has other plans. He brushes past me with the arrogance of a man used to taking up space, stepping into my office uninvited.

"I like this room just fine."

Boris' gaze sweeps over my office, taking in the luxurious furnishings and expensive art with a sardonic sneer. "Quite the palace you've built for yourself here, Ivan," he remarks in Russian, his voice dripping with a blend of envy and disdain. "Seems you've done well for yourself."

His eyes linger on a particularly expensive piece of artwork, and his lips curl into a mocking smile. "Opulence suits you, doesn't it? A far cry from the back alleys and shadowy deals of Moscow. But no matter how high you climb, remember, the roots always show."

I stand at the threshold, a silent barrier between Boris and the world I've built here. My mind races with the possible reasons behind Boris' presence, along with the potential threat he poses not just to me, but to Julie, as well. Her involvement, even as a bystander, complicates things in a way I'm not comfortable with.

As Boris' eyes linger on her, I feel a protective instinct kick in, one that I've never associated with my professional demeanor. She's my assistant, but in this moment she represents something more, something that Boris and his world should have no part of.

I need to control the situation, keep Julie out of whatever Boris has planned.

Quickly, I introduce her, "This is my assistant." I shoot her a look, a silent message. "And she doesn't need to be here for this conversation."

Attuned to my thoughts, she promptly asks, "Will there be anything else, Mr. Stepanov?"

I respond with a firm negative, masking the turmoil inside me with a façade of indifference. Julie then says, "I'm taking the rest of the day off." Her voice is steady, but there's an undercurrent of uncertainty that only I notice.

I let her go, maintaining my stoic expression as my mind races with dangerous possibilities.

As she leaves, I turn back to Boris and his men, my mind shifting gears. I need to deal with this right now, handle whatever it is that brought him here. His gaze on Julie lingers a moment too long as she walks away. "Nice assistant you have there, Ivan. And that ass..." he says, leering openly.

I clench my jaw, forcing myself to keep my composure. Responding with anger will only escalate the situation, give Boris the reaction he's looking for. But I can't let it slide.

"She's unavailable," I state firmly, my voice edged with a warning. "And there will be no talk of my employees in such a disrespectful manner."

Boris snorts with a smirk, as if amused.

In my mind, Julie is already mine, even if she hasn't agreed to marry me yet. The thought of him or anyone else ogling her is intolerable.

Shifting the focus, I ask, "Why are you here, Boris? It's been a long time." My tone is direct, cutting through his insinuations and lewd remarks.

He seems to enjoy dragging out the moment, reveling in the discomfort he's causing. "How about some vodka, Ivan? For old times' sake?" he suggests, nodding toward my small office bar. "Perfect way to start the day."

Reluctantly, I pour him and Sergei—who has made himself comfortable on my couch—a drink while carefully maintaining my stoic demeanor. I hand each a glass, and immediately after Boris takes a sip, he gets to the point. "The Bratva needs your expertise on a few matters."

My response is immediate and unequivocal. "No," I say sharply, without needing to know the details. "I left that life behind me, Boris, and I have no intention of reentering it. You knew that when I left Russia."

His eyes narrow slightly, but he doesn't seem surprised by my refusal. He's testing the waters, probing for weaknesses, but I'm not the same man I was when I worked for him. I've built a new life, a legitimate one, and I won't allow him or anyone else to drag me back into the shadows of my past.

The Bratva might have been a part of who I was, but it's not who I am now. And it's certainly not a world I want Julie to be exposed to, even peripherally. My refusal is as much for her protection as it is for my own resolve to stay out of that life.

As Boris sips his vodka, eyeing me with a mix of calculation and amusement, I stand firm. My decision is made, and no amount of persuasion or coercion will change it. I've fought too hard to become the man I am today, and I won't let the ghosts of my past threaten that.

He chuckles, a sound that grates on my nerves. "Ivan, you know how it is. Once Bratva, always Bratva," he says, a smugness in his tone that I find particularly irksome.

I stand my ground, my voice firm. "Anton Mikhailov released me from my duties. I am no longer bound to the organization."

But Boris waves off my words as if they are mere inconveniences. "Mikhailov did not have the final say. I did not agree to your release. You are expected to follow orders."

His words are a stark reminder of the ties that still bind me to a world I desperately want to forget. "I've made a new life, Boris. I am not at your beck and call," I retort, my frustration growing.

Boris, seemingly unfazed, prepares to leave, his parting words hanging heavy in the air, a threat disguised as a casual remark. "I'll be in touch with instructions for your first job," he says with a cocky smirk, implying an inevitable return to the dark dealings I've sworn off.

As the men leave, closing the door behind them, I'm left with a sense of foreboding. Boris' visit and his expectations are a complication I don't need, especially now, as I'm on the verge of starting a new chapter of my life. A chapter that, I hope, includes Julie as my wife.

The word 'wife' resonates in my mind. Julie hasn't agreed to my proposal yet, but more than ever, I feel the urgency to protect her, to shield her from the dangerous world that's just barged back in.

My mind begins to strategize. I need to handle my old boss and his expectations while keeping Julie safe and oblivious to the threats that loom over us. I cannot, I will not, let my past entangle with the future I hope to build with her.

Boris' words, "I'll be in touch," echo in my mind. I know the Bratva's reach is long and their memory even longer. But I've battled with them before and I've come out stronger. This time will be no different, except now, I have something more to fight for.

The Bratva may think they can control me, but they're about to learn that Ivan Stepanov is not a man who bows to anyone's will—not anymore.

CHAPTER 10

JULIE

The magnitude of Ivan's proposal continues to weigh heavily on my mind as I sit in my apartment staring blankly at the wall.

Several hours of introspection have brought me no closer to a decision. The thought of being locked in a marriage with Ivan for a minimum of twenty years is terrifying. I might have a husband and a child, but I would not have love.

In a desperate attempt to find a silver lining, I imagine my life as the kind of romcom it's starting to resemble. Maybe Ivan and I will fall in love once we're married and building a fake life together.

Who am I kidding? I dismiss the thought almost as soon as it forms. Ivan is all business, through and through. His world revolves around deals, negotiations, and cold, hard logic. Feelings and human emotions don't seem to have a place in his life. He's a man driven by ambition and professionalism, not romance.

But then I remember last night. That moment in his office, how close he stepped to me with that peculiarly profound look in his eyes. There was a hint of something more than just lust. Maybe. Or maybe it was just lust... Either way, lust isn't love. It's a fleeting, physical reaction, not the foundation for a lifelong commitment.

My mind spins, tangled in a web of what-ifs and maybes. The more I think about it, the more I realize there's only one person who can help me sort through this mess and that's my Aunt Barb, the woman who raised me after my father killed my mother.

I need her perspective, her wisdom. She's always had a way of cutting through the noise, of helping me see the heart of the matter. And right now, I need that clarity more than ever.

Reaching for my phone, I dial her number—texting got me in trouble last time. My heart feels heavy with the gravity of the decision before me. This isn't just about a job or a career move. It's about my life, my future, and potentially, the creation of a new family.

We meet at Murray's—our favorite deli—a cozy spot that's seen many of our heart-to-hearts over the years. Barb, with her free-spirited aura and artist's sensibility, is the polar opposite of me. She's my mom's twin sister, but you'd never guess we were related from our personalities.

Her hair is a wild mane of curls, and she's wearing a flowy, bohemian dress that looks like one of her canvases come to life.

Barb can always tell when something's up with me, and today's no different. She eyes me with a knowing look as she sips her coffee.

"Spill it, Jules. You never miss work. What's got you so antsy?"

God, where to begin?

I recount the tale of the accidentally erotic message left for Ivan, watching Barb's reaction closely. And then I follow up with his... reply.

At first, her eyebrows rise in surprise, a hand flying to her mouth in a gesture of mock horror. But as the story unfolds, her expression shifts. The corners of her eyes crinkle with amusement, and soon, she's laughing, a deep, hearty laugh that fills the deli. Her laughter is infectious, spreading warmth and lightness, transforming my embarrassment into something almost bearable.

"It sounds like it could be a scene from one of these popular shows currently streaming, Jules!" Barb exclaims, wiping a tear from the corner of her eye. It's one of the things I love most about her; her knack for turning life's awkward moments into anecdotes to be laughed at over coffee.

Emboldened by her reaction, I delve into the heavier part of my story.

"But that's not all," I say, and I watch as Barb's expression sobers, her artist's eyes sharpening with interest. She leans in, her bracelets jangling softly, signaling her full attention.

I tell her about Ivan's proposal, his unexpected offer of marriage and funding for my nonprofit. I detail the terms, the prenup, and his cool, business-like approach to the whole thing.

"Honey, that's... quite a proposition," she finally says.

As she digests the information, I can see the wheels turning in her head. Barb's always had a gift for seeing the bigger picture, for understanding the artistry in life's chaos.

"It's a lot to think about," she adds before her eyebrows shoot up, as if something's just occurred to her. "To be honest, it sounds like he's trying to buy you, honey."

I nod, my fork playing with the salad on my plate. "I know, right? That's exactly what I thought. But the idea of getting my nonprofit off the ground, doing something good with his money... I have to admit it's tempting."

Barb leans back in her chair, studying me like I'm one of her paintings. "But at what cost, Julie? You're talking about marriage, kids, a whole life with a man who sees this as a transaction."

I sigh, feeling the weight of her words. "I know, I know. It's just that this could be a chance to make a real difference, to honor Mom's memory in a big way."

We sit in silence for a moment, the deli bustling around us. Barb's always been the one to encourage my dreams, to push me to pursue my passions. But this is different. This is about the rest of my life, about bringing another human into the world.

She reaches across the table, her hand covering mine. "Whatever you decide, Jules, make sure it's what you truly want, not just what's convenient or tempting."

I nod, her words sinking in.

"Jules, your need to start this nonprofit, to honor your mother, it's noble. She would be so proud of you. But" she pauses, choosing her words carefully, "are you going to be okay being in a loveless marriage? A marriage where the only expectation of you is to have a child?"

Her question hangs in the air between us. It's the heart of the matter, the crux of my dilemma. I open my mouth to respond, but words fail me. The truth is, I don't know if I'm okay with it. The idea of a loveless marriage, a relationship built on convenience and business, goes against everything I've ever dreamed of.

"I don't know," I finally admit, my voice barely above a whisper.

Barb gives me a sympathetic smile, then stands up. "I'm going to the restroom. Sit with your thoughts for a minute."

Left alone, I try to imagine what my life with Ivan would look like. There would be the obvious logistics of the arrangement concerning the marriage, the child. And then there's the fact that we'd have to have sex for me to get pregnant. Unsurprisingly, that thought doesn't bother me at all. In fact, the idea of being intimate with Ivan sends a thrill through me. He's undeniably sexy, a man of intensity and passion, and I have no doubts he'd be a good lover. And after that insane foreplay, Lord knows I'm dying to get the full treatment from this man.

The mutual attraction is undeniable. I've seen the way he looks at me, the brief flashes of desire in his eyes long before he showed up at my door. It's more than just professional interest.

The thought of being close to him, of sharing a physical intimacy that would result in a new life being brought into this world, is strangely exciting. It's a far cry from the romantic, love-filled relationship I've always imagined and dreamed about, but there's an undeniable pull, a chemistry between the two of us that can't be ignored. It's damn near palpable. I still quiver from his touch.

But is chemistry enough? Is the promise of financial stability and the opportunity to start my nonprofit worth the trade-off of a marriage without love?

These are the questions swirling in my mind as I sit in the deli, my salad untouched, my coffee growing cold. It's a decision that's about more than just practicality or passion; it's about what I want my life to be, what I value, and what I'm willing to sacrifice.

As I wait for Barb to return, I realize that this decision isn't just about choosing a path; it's about defining who I am and what I stand for. And that's a choice that requires more than just logic or desire. It requires a deep understanding of myself and my dreams.

By the time my aunt returns, I've worked myself into a state that's half-determination, half-delirium. She slides back into her seat, eyeing me with curiosity.

"OK, thoughts?" She grins and leans in.

"What about the day-to-day stuff?" I blurt out, my tone one of exasperation. "Will we spend our evenings together like a real married couple? Go on dates, take trips? Or will it be more like, 'Hey, honey, I'm off to run a multinational corporation, see you at the next board meeting.'"

Barb chuckles, clearly amused by my dramatic rendition. "You do have a way with words, Jules."

I lean back in my chair, my mind racing. "He's all business, Aunt Barb. I mean, the man could probably turn a romantic dinner into a shareholders' meeting."

"What about last night?"

"It may have been no more than a slip," I say, probably lying to myself. If I'm to do this marriage thing, taking our intimacy too deep might be trouble in the long run. If I convince myself that this is strictly business, I could actually do it. I think. "I really believe he just wants me to pop out a kid and help him raise it, and that will be the extent of our dealings with one another."

Barb nods, her expression thoughtful. "But is that enough for you? That's the real question."

I pause, considering it again. "If it means I can start my nonprofit years sooner, helping women and children escape abusive situations, I think I can handle playing house with Ivan Stepanov."

Barb raises an eyebrow, a silent question hanging in the air.

I throw my hands up, a mock gesture of surrender. "Fine, I'll admit that there's something about him. But," I add quickly, "that's not why I'm considering it. It's about the nonprofit, the good I can do."

Barb smiles, a glint of pride in her eyes. "You always were one to make sacrifices for the greater good."

I take a deep breath, feeling like I'm teetering on the edge of the biggest decision of my life.

CHAPTER 11

IVAN

Two days after my meeting with Boris, I find myself walking to the courthouse, accompanied by my younger brother, Fyodor.

Dressed in a suit that's perfectly tailored to his lanky frame, Fyodor is the antithesis of me in many ways. Where I am reserved and businesslike, he is charming, personable, and talkative. He never got involved with the Bratva, enjoying the spoils of my efforts from a safe distance through more typical employment.

At our mother's insistence—and with my support—he went to college and now heads the IT department of my company. His light brown hair is styled in a way that's casual yet professional, and his easy smile is a stark contrast to my usual stern expression.

As we approach the courthouse, Fyodor nudges me.

"Are you sure about this?" he asks for what must be the hundredth time. His voice is laced with concern and a touch of disbelief. "Marrying your assistant in a business transaction to get an heir is a bit extreme, don't you think?"

I glance at him, my expression unreadable. "It's the most efficient solution," I reply, my tone firm. The decision hasn't come easily, but I've weighed the options, and this makes the most sense—for me, for my company, and for the legacy I intend to leave.

Fyodor shakes his head, his expression one of exasperation mixed with amusement. "You and your efficiency. There are other ways, you know. You could date, find a girlfriend, do it the normal way."

The idea of dating, of going through the motions of a romantic relationship, seems unnecessarily complicated and time-consuming. I've never been one for the social intricacies of dating, and with the current complications in my life, it's even less appealing.

"Finding a girlfriend who isn't interested in me for my money has proved to be impossible," I tell him, my voice tinged with a hint of cynicism. "Every woman I've met so far has been a gold digger."

The reality of my situation is stark, and perhaps a bit jaded. My wealth and status attract a certain type of attention from women—they are more interested in the material benefits than in me as a person. It's a truth I've come to accept, one that's shaped my approach to personal relationships.

"But Julie isn't like that," I continue, the conviction in my voice unwavering. "The prenup is in place to protect us both, and in this arrangement, we both get what we want. It's straightforward and uncomplicated."

Fyodor chuckles, a light-hearted sound that seems out of place considering the seriousness of our conversation. "You really do have a talent for turning everything into a business transaction, bro," he teases.

"This is the best way," I state again, stopping in front of the courthouse steps. "Julie understands the arrangement. It's mutually beneficial."

Fyodor sighs, running a hand through his hair. "I just hope you're not making a mistake. Marriage is more than just a contract and a child, or it should be. There are emotions involved, feelings, like *love*."

I pause, considering the word. It's not often I allow myself to contemplate such intangibles. "Love is a luxury I cannot afford right now. This is about the company, about securing a future. Julie understands the stakes, the practicality of it all."

"I get the practical side, Ivan, but marriage is also about companionship, about finding someone who, well, someone who complements you, not just fulfills a role."

His words strike a chord, unearthing a sliver of doubt I've been careful to bury. "Julie is competent, intelligent. She's more than capable of fulfilling this role. And in return, she gets to achieve her dreams as well. It's a fair exchange."

"Just don't shortchange yourself in this deal, Ivan," Fyodor advises, his tone softening. "You deserve more than just a business partner for a wife. You deserve happiness, too."

I glance at him, a brief flicker of vulnerability crossing my otherwise composed exterior. "Happiness is a fleeting thing,

Fyodor. What I need is stability, for me and for Stepanov Holdings. That's my priority."

My brother nods, accepting my decision but not entirely convinced. "Just remember, life is unpredictable. Sometimes, what starts as a transaction can become something more, something unexpected. Be open to that possibility."

We enter the courthouse, our steps echoing in the quiet hallway. The weight of the decision I've made settles over me. This marriage, this arrangement with Julie, it's an unexpected new chapter in my life, one that I'm entering with my eyes wide open.

I'm about to pause and look around when my gaze lands on her. She's waiting inside, and the sight of her instantly shifts my focus. All thoughts of business arrangements and negotiations fade away, and it's just her, the woman who could soon be my wife.

As we approach Julie, the sight of her takes my breath away. She stands there in a simple white dress that accentuates her curves with an elegant subtlety. The simplicity of her attire only enhances her natural beauty, making her stand out even more in the stark environment of the courthouse.

Fyodor, never one to hold back his thoughts, leans in and whispers, "She's stunning."

I don't respond to his comment. Words seem inadequate at the moment. My eyes are fixed on Julie, and I'm taking in every detail, from the way her dress cascades toward the floor to the confident, yet slightly nervous tilt of her head. It's a moment of realization for me, a dawning understanding that this arrangement, this marriage, is about more than just a contract and a mutual benefit.

Julie, in her understated elegance, represents something I hadn't fully acknowledged until now. She's not just a means to an heir or a partner in a practical agreement. She's a woman of grace and beauty, someone who's managed to captivate me in ways I hadn't anticipated.

And she's not alone. A middle-aged woman dressed in flowing, bohemian-chic clothes is with her. As they draw near, I can see the resemblance. The other woman is likely family.

I pause for a moment, allowing myself to truly take her in. "It's good to see you, Julie," I say, my voice softer than usual. "You look lovely."

She meets my gaze, a faint blush coloring her cheeks. "Thank you, Ivan. You look quite distinguished yourself," she replies, her voice steady but with an undercurrent that suggests a depth of feeling she's keeping carefully in check.

There's a momentary silence as we stand there, the air between us charged with an unspoken intensity and a hint of uncertainty.

Fyodor is the first to initiate introductions. He steps forward, extending his hand toward Julie's companion with a congenial smile. "Hi. I'm Fyodor, Ivan's brother," he greets warmly. "Pleasure to meet you."

The woman, whose vibrant aura contrasts with the formal setting, returns the handshake. "I'm Barbara, Julie's aunt," she responds, her tone friendly yet filled with curiosity. "But everyone just calls me Barb. Nice to meet you too."

Barb then turns toward me, extending her hand confidently. "You must be Ivan," she says, her eyes holding a glint of interest.

I take her hand. "Indeed, I am Ivan Stepanov. It's a pleasure, Barb," I reply, my tone polite yet reserved.

Julie, standing beside me, watches the exchange with an unreadable expression. "Barb has been a big support," she adds, her voice carrying a note of fondness.

I nod, acknowledging the sentiment. "I can see that. It's always good to have family around."

"Well," I say, releasing Barb's hand and gesturing to the nearby courtroom where the proceedings are set to occur. "Shall we?"

"I suppose we shall," Julie says.

As we step into the courtroom, the heavy door closing behind us with a definitive thud, I steal one last glance at Julie. In the sterile light, she's a welcome presence in a world of legal formalities and repetitious procedures.

"Ready for this?" I ask, my voice a low whisper that only she can hear.

Julie nods, her eyes meeting mine with a resolve that mirrors my own. "As ready as I'll ever be," she replies, her voice laced with a courage that I can't help but admire.

With that, we turn to face the judge, side by side, stepping into a future neither of us could have predicted. It's a new beginning for both of us, untraditional yet meticulously planned, and underlined by a current of something raw and uncharted.

As the judge begins to speak, the reality of our decision anchors itself. For the first time, I find myself embracing the uncertainty of it all, intrigued by the possibilities it holds.

CHAPTER 12

JULIE

The wedding—if I can even call it that—wraps up in a cool ten minutes. It feels more like a business meeting that just happened to include exchanging rings. Ivan slips a simple gold band onto my finger, its weight foreign and oddly significant. In return, I slide the matching band onto his. He picked them both out, of course. Practical, no fuss.

When we say, "I do," the words echo in the courtroom, sounding too loud, too formal. Ivan presses his lips against mine, a chaste, brief contact that sends an unexpected shiver down my spine. It's over before I fully register it, but the sensation lingers, a ghost of a touch that leaves me more confused about my feelings than ever.

As the judge pronounces us husband and wife, I can't help but steal another glance at Ivan. He's looking every bit the embodiment of a modern-day prince in his impeccably tailored suit. The fabric seems to cling to him in all the right places, accentuating his broad shoulders and the lean strength of his frame. The suit, a deep navy blue, makes him appear even more commanding and impossibly sexy.

As we step away from the judge's bench, I turn to my new husband. "So what now?" I ask, trying to keep my voice light, masking the whirlwind of thoughts in my head.

Ivan is all business, as usual. "I have a car waiting for us outside," he says.

"A car? Are we going on a honeymoon, or do you have a meeting?" The words slip out before I can stop them, my attempt at humor masking the surrealness of the situation.

As Barb and I say our farewells in the courthouse lobby, I can't help but notice the concern etched on her face, her eyes reflecting both love and worry. She pulls me into a warm embrace, her arms wrapping around me with a motherly tenderness. "Julie, you can always come to me, anytime, day or night, if you need anything," she whispers, her voice heavy. "You know that, right?"

I nod, swallowing the lump forming in my throat. "I know, Aunt Barb. Thank you," I manage to say.

She then turns to Ivan, her gaze piercing, protective. "You better take good care of her, Ivan. She's precious, and I'm entrusting her to you."

Ivan meets her gaze steadily, a flicker of respect in his eyes. "I assure you, Barb, Julie will be well taken care of," he says, his voice firm, leaving no room for doubt.

Barb studies him for a moment longer, as if weighing his words, then finally nods, seemingly satisfied with his promise. She turns back to me, kissing my cheeks softly. "Remember what I said, darling."

As we part ways, Fyodor steps in with his easy charm and a smile that lightens the mood. "Welcome to the family, Julie," he says, his voice warm and welcoming, though a hint of hesitation lingers beneath his cheerful demeanor.

He doesn't seem entirely convinced about the nature of our union, but his friendly disposition is a stark contrast to Ivan's more reserved manner. "Let me walk you to your car, Barb," he offers, extending his arm to her in a gentlemanly gesture.

Once alone with Ivan, the air shifts. The presence of others had provided a buffer, a distraction from the reality of our situation. But now it's just him and me, a husband and wife in the most unconventional sense.

As we reach the curb, a sleek car glides to a smooth stop in front of us. The driver, dressed in a crisp uniform, quickly hops out and opens the door with a practiced air of professionalism.

Stepping inside, I'm immediately struck by the lavish interior—a bottle of champagne along with two flutes are chilling in a silver bucket and a small charcuterie board arranged with an assortment of cheeses and meats sit beside it, all elegantly displayed. It's all very Ivan; efficient luxury without a hint of ostentation.

Ivan follows, sliding into the seat opposite me with an ease that speaks of his familiarity with this kind of luxury. He reaches for the champagne bottle, his movements precise and practiced. With a deft flick of his wrist, he pops the cork, the sound cutting through the quiet of the car.

Pouring two glasses of the sparkling liquid, he hands one to me. Our fingers brush briefly, sending a jolt through me. It's a simple touch, but in the confined space of the car, it feels intimate, charged. A reminder of the fire still blazing between us.

He raises his glass, clinking it gently against mine. "To our partnership," he says, his deep voice resonating in the small space.

His eyes lock onto mine as he takes a sip, and I feel an inexplicable pull, an observance that goes beyond the clink of our glasses. It's unsettling and yet oddly thrilling at the same time. I want to gulp down the champagne, let the bubbles ease the bundle of nerves in my stomach, but I resist. I take a small, measured sip instead, trying to match his composure.

The taste is exquisite, a perfect blend of flavors that dances on my tongue, but it's not enough to distract me from the man sitting across from me. The reality of our situation, the enormity of the decision I've made, starts to sink in.

Ivan's unexpected question catches me off guard. "Which do you prefer, mountains or the beach?" he asks, his tone casual, as if we're just two acquaintances making small talk.

I can't help but laugh. "That's quite the icebreaker question," I say, amused by the sudden shift from formalities to something that feels more like a first date query.

He simply smiles, a rare expression that softens his usually stern features, and lifts an eyebrow in silent encouragement for me to answer.

"Definitely the beach," I reply, still smiling. "There's something about the sound of the waves and the feel of sand underfoot that's relaxing."

As I speak, Ivan pulls out his phone, his fingers moving swiftly over the screen. He seems absorbed in whatever he's typing, but then he looks up, meeting my eyes with a gaze that's both intense and unreadable.

"What's going on?" I ask, curiosity piqued. It's not like him to be distracted during a conversation, especially not on a day as significant as this one.

"The company plane will be taking us to Bora Bora for the week," he says, as if announcing a routine business trip.

I blink, the words taking a moment to sink in. "Bora Bora? As in, the tropical paradise Bora Bora?" My voice rises in disbelief. This isn't just a getaway; it's a full-blown honeymoon destination, one most people only dream about. Including me.

Ivan nods, a trace of something similar to satisfaction flickering in his eyes. "Yes, that Bora Bora. Consider it a celebration of our new partnership."

The car suddenly feels like it's spinning, even though we're moving in a perfectly straight line. Bora Bora. I've only seen in it travel magazines or on the Travel channel, a dream destination for a honeymoon I never imagined I'd have, especially not like this.

My mind races, trying to process this new development. It's a chance to escape, to breathe in new air and maybe to better understand this complex man sitting across from me.

"Wow, Ivan, that's incredibly generous," I manage, still reeling from the surprise. "I don't even know what to say."

"You don't have to say anything," he replies, his voice steady.

As I sit back, sipping my bubbly, the reality of it all begins to settle in.

I'm going to Bora Bora with Ivan Stepanov.

My boss.

My husband.

The thought sends a thrill of excitement mixed with a twinge of apprehension through me. This trip, this unexpected honeymoon, could be the start of something new, something I hadn't dared to ever hope for.

CHAPTER 13

JULIE

As the sleek car cruises through the city, the revelation about Bora Bora leaves me reeling. "Wait, hold on a second," I blurt, my voice climbing an octave. "I'm not prepared for this! I don't have the right clothes for a freaking tropical paradise, and..." my eyes flash... "what about Kiki?"

Ivan raises an eyebrow. "Kiki?"

"My cat! I didn't arrange for anyone to feed her."

My mind is a whirlwind of logistics and sheer panic. The idea of a week in the tropics, while undeniably tempting, throws me completely off balance. I'm mentally rifling through my wardrobe, trying to imagine what I can pull together for a beach vacation. And then there's Kiki, my furball of judgment and affection, who definitely won't appreciate being left to her own devices.

In the midst of my spiraling thoughts, Ivan reaches over and plucks my phone out of my hand. I stop mid-rant, my mouth hanging open in surprise.

"Hey!" I exclaim, a mix of indignation and confusion coloring my tone. "What are you doing?"

He doesn't even bat an eyelash. With the calmness of a man used to handling crises, he starts scrolling through my contacts. "Who takes care of Kiki when you're not around?" he asks, his focus still on my phone.

"Um, my neighbor, Mrs. Dalca. She's a total cat whisperer, swears she was a feline in her past life," I reply, still slightly taken aback by his direct approach.

Without missing a beat, Ivan finds Mrs. Dalca's number and dials it.

"Mrs. Dalca? Hello, this is Ivan Stepanov, Julie's husband," he says. "We've had an unexpected trip come up, and we were wondering if you could take care of Kiki for the week."

He listens for a moment, then a small smile plays on his lips. "Yes, Bora Bora," he confirms, as if it's the most normal thing in the world to jet off to an exotic location at a moment's notice. "Much appreciated. And don't worry, you'll be well compensated. Yes, thank you."

I watch him handle the situation with an ease that's both infuriating and impressive. The way he takes charge, solving problems with a phone call, is classic Ivan. And as much as I want to be annoyed with him for invading my personal space, I can't help but feel a twinge of gratitude, and maybe something else.

"Everything's taken care of," he says, handing back my phone. "Mrs. Dalca will look after Kiki. And as for your wardrobe," he continues, turning to face me, his dark eyes locking with mine, "I've arranged for a personal shopper to meet us at the hotel. They'll provide everything you need for the week."

My mouth is suddenly dry, and the close confines of the car appear to be closing in, his presence seemingly filling up the space. "You what?" I manage to stammer, my brain struggling to keep up. "A personal shopper?"

He nods, the corners of his mouth lifting in a half-smile that's infuriatingly sexy. "Of course. I wouldn't expect you to go unprepared."

As Ivan smoothly continues, explaining how everything has been taken care of, I find myself oscillating between irritation and awe. "Fyodor walked Barb to her car, just to let her know what's going on. Between him and Barb, everything at home will be taken care of," he says, his voice calm and reassuring.

I'm still trying to process this whirlwind of organization and consideration. Part of me, the part that likes to be in control, to make my own decisions, is irked. I'm not used to having choices made for me, having my life neatly planned out by someone else, even if it is just for a week.

It feels like I'm being swept along by a current I can't control, one that's both exhilarating and unnerving.

But then there's the other part of me, the part that's secretly thrilled by this grand gesture. No one has ever surprised me like this, whisked me away to a tropical paradise on a whim. It's like something out of a movie, and I can't help but feel a rush of excitement, a giddy anticipation for what lies ahead.

"Thank you, Ivan," I say, my voice tinged with a mixture of gratitude and disbelief. "I've never been to Bora Bora. Actually, I've never been anywhere like it. Hell, I can't even remember the last time I've been out of the city."

He turns to me, his expression softening ever so slightly. "From now on, you can go anywhere you like," he tells me, and there's a sincerity in his voice that catches me off guard.

Leaning back in the plush seat, I take another sip of champagne, the bubbles tickling my nose. The lightheaded feeling isn't just from the alcohol; it's also from the excitement of what lies ahead and how different my life is about to become.

Growing up, Barb and I were never destitute, but we certainly weren't jet-setting around the world. Barb's art was beautiful, but it wasn't until my high school years that her pieces started selling for the kind of money that changed things for us. Our trips were always within driving distance, modest adventures that were rich in adventure and fun, but not in luxury.

Now I am in a limousine with Ivan, heading to an airport where a private plane awaits to take us to one of the most beautiful places on earth. It's overwhelming; a complete juxtaposition to the life I've known.

The moment I step onto the company plane, my excitement goes to another level. It's like stepping into the pages of a glossy, high-end travel magazine.

The interior is a masterclass in luxury and elegance—plush, leather seats that look more comfortable than my couch at home, glossy wood panels, and soft, ambient lighting that creates a serene atmosphere. It's spacious, more so than any plane I've ever been on, with a seating area that resembles a chic, high-end lounge.

"I didn't think I'd ever be a passenger on the company plane," I say as I roam around, touching the soft leather, admiring the sleek design, every detail perfect and luxurious.

Ivan watches me with a small, knowing smile. "There are many things about the company you're yet to experience," he replies, his voice laced with amusement.

As I continue to explore, a team of impeccably dressed staff bustles around us, efficiently packing our things into the storage compartments and ensuring we're comfortably situated. They move with precision and grace, making the whole process seem effortless.

Once we're airborne, the gentle hum of the engines creates a soothing backdrop. "The flight is quite long. Feel free to take a nap or watch television if you like." Ivan sweeps his hand toward the interior as he speaks.

Then he nods at a door at the other end of the cabin. "There's a bed through there," he adds casually. "If you need a rest."

A bed. On the plane. My insides do more than quake; they do a full-blown salsa dance. The idea of a bed in this confined space with Ivan sends my imagination into overdrive. It's both terrifying and tantalizing, a forbidden thought that I can't seem to push away. Technically speaking, not really forbidden anymore, though, is it?

I nod, trying to appear nonchalant, but inside, I'm a whirlwind of nerves and excitement. "Thanks, I might just do that," I say, my voice a little too high-pitched.

I settle into one of the luxurious seats, trying to focus on the TV screen in front of me. But my mind keeps wandering back to that door, to what lies beyond it. The thought of lying in that bed, the soft sheets, the quiet hum of the plane... Ivan, just a few steps away.

I take a deep breath, trying to calm the flurry of thoughts and emotions swirling inside me. This is all new territory, uncharted waters that I'm navigating without a map.

The champagne and the gentle hum of the plane have me feeling bolder than usual. As I stand to walk past Ivan, I make sure my hip brushes his shoulder ever so slightly. It's a small, deliberate gesture, a silent acknowledgment of the sexual tension that's been simmering between us.

Ivan's reaction is immediate. His hand shoots out, catching mine, halting my movement. Our eyes lock, his gaze intense and questioning. "Did you do that on purpose?" he asks, his voice low, a hint of anticipation lacing his words.

I don't answer. Instead, I hold his gaze, letting my eyes speak for me. The unspoken message is clear—yes, it was on purpose. I'm done with pretending, done with ignoring the attraction that's been building between us. Those orgasms he gave me require a rematch. Pronto.

Ivan seems to understand. He stands up, and in one fluid motion, he's right in front of me, his presence overwhelming. He pulls me close, one hand firm on my back, his other hand gently tilting my chin up. "I've been thinking about kissing you since I saw you on the courthouse steps," he confesses, his voice a rumbling whisper.

We never actually kissed. That night, he ate me whole, but our lips never met...

The admission sends a shiver through me. I've wanted this, fantasized about it, but hearing him say it out loud makes it real. The anticipation is almost too much to bear.

He kisses me. It's not a gentle, questioning kiss. It's powerful, demanding, a floodgate opening after being held back for too long. His lips are firm against mine, insistent, and I respond with equal fervor. My arms wrap around his neck, pulling him closer, deepening the kiss.

The pent-up desire, the tension, all of it comes pouring out in one kiss. Ivan's hands roam over my back, pulling me even closer, his touch igniting a fire that's been smoldering for far too long.

As we finally break apart, panting, the reality of what just happened hits me. I've just kissed my boss, now my husband, the man I've been drooling over for months. And it was everything I'd imagined and more.

We stand there, inches apart, breathing heavily. The look in Ivan's eyes is one I've never seen before—raw, exposed, and utterly captivating. It's a look that says this is just the beginning, that there's so much more to explore, to discover beyond that handful of minutes on my couch.

In the quiet luxury of the plane, on our way to a tropical paradise, everything seems possible. The rules, the expectations, the roles we've played all fall away, leaving just Ivan and me, and the undeniable truth of our attraction.

CHAPTER 14

IVAN

We move toward the bedroom, closing the door behind us. Slowly, with a reverence that surprises even me, I gently slide my fingers beneath the straps of her dress, allowing it to slowly fall away, revealing skin that's soft and inviting under my fingertips. I'd missed this. I've been dying to touch her again. Her breath quickens, her chest rising and falling with anticipation.

There's a nervous excitement in her eyes, a willingness to explore the unknown territory we're venturing into.

I sense her nervousness but also her willingness, her trust in me to guide her through this experience. It's a responsibility I don't take lightly. This isn't just the whim of a hot moment, a response to a saucy text. This is our first night as husband and wife. With every touch, every kiss, I'm careful to gauge her reactions, ensuring she's comfortable and that this is what she wants.

As her last garment slips away, leaving her exposed and vulnerable, I take a moment to appreciate her beauty in this specific context. My woman. The dim light casts her in a soft glow, highlighting the contours of her body. She's stunning, a vision of desire and openness that captivates me entirely.

Julie stands before me, the lights casting a gentle glow on her. I'm struck by the sheer beauty of her form. Her skin is soft and luminous, a canvas of natural grace that invites my touch. Her shoulders are delicately curved, leading down to arms that have a subtle strength to them. Her breasts are full and round, her nipples small and pink. My gaze moves down, all along her figure, down to the thatch of blonde hair above her womanhood. There's a tingling sensation in my upper lip, a remnant of that night on her couch.

God, I want her.

"Come here," I growl, my voice low and laced with desire. As we approach the bed, each step feels charged with an exhilarating anticipation.

Julie's gaze meets mine, a mixture of excitement and a hint of apprehension dancing in her eyes. "Ivan," she whispers, her voice a velvet caress that sends shivers down my spine.

She lays back and I climb onto the bed, my body hovering over hers. The proximity heightens the intensity of the moment, each breath we take mingling in the charged air between us.

"You're beautiful," I say, not just as a compliment, but as a simple statement of truth. My hands gently trace the contours of her body, exploring the landscape that's both familiar and still so new.

Julie's response is a soft sigh, her body responding to my touch with a subtle arching up toward me. "And you are too damn handsome for your own good," she breathes out, her hands reaching up to caress my face.

I savor the moments before we make love, drinking in the sight of her naked body beneath me. I'm hard as stone, my cock throbbing with an eagerness to be buried inside her. Julie reaches down, wrapping her slender fingers around my manhood, a small smile forming on her full, luscious lips.

"Tell me what you want," I command, lowering myself to kiss her, the tip of my cock grazing against her slick folds.

"You. I want you." She flashes me a sly smile.

"Then show me."

She strokes me a bit more, the backs of her nails grazing against the underside of my cock. Julie takes hold of me once more, pulling me into her. I feel her lips spread, followed by the warmth of her pussy as my head pushes in.

"Oh.... Oh, wow..." she gasps.

The words are carried by her hot breath as I sink into her balls deep. She's tight, but with a slow, deep plunge, I stretch her out, reach her depth. She moans, squirming underneath me as she wraps her legs around my waist, guiding me in as far as I can go.

I lower myself as I pull back and push into her again. She opens those gorgeous eyes, looking right at me. She's innocent and vulnerable, but there's a sly, animal hunger to the way she regards me, as if she's ready to show me her wild side.

I build my pace, pushing into her over and over, her warm walls gripping me.

"God," she moans. "If only you knew how many times I've fantasized about this."

Her words turn me on even more than I already am.

"I know one of them, at least," I say with a mischievous grin, referring to the overheard self-pleasuring episode that started our little arrangement.

She laughs, but her amused expression quickly turns back to one of serious, focused passion. I plunge into her again and again, her hair splaying out around her head like a fan of fire, her breasts bouncing with the power of each thrust.

As the intensity between us builds, I stay focused on Julie, attuned to her every reaction, every breath. My movements become more deliberate, each stroke designed to heighten her pleasure, to bring her closer to the edge. I can feel her body tensing, the anticipation building within her.

"Let go, Julie," I whisper, my voice low and encouraging as I slip a hand between us and draw deliberate circles on her swollen clit.

Her response is immediate and uninhibited. She arches beneath me, a symphony of soft moans and quickened breaths filling the space between us. I continue to move, my own desire mirroring hers, each moment drawing us closer to a shared climax.

Finally, she crosses that threshold, a wave of release washing over her. Her body shudders beneath me, a beautiful, raw expression of pleasure that drives me to my own edge. I feel her pussy tighten around my shaft, the intensity in her eyes urging me on.

With a few more purposeful thrusts, I join her in that exquisite release. It's a moment of profound connection, of two people lost in the sheer intensity of the experience. Our breaths mingle, our bodies intertwined in the aftermath, basking in the glow of a deeply shared intimacy.

Lying there in the serene afterglow, as the hum of the airplane engines blends into the background, I turn to Julie, a playful smile touching my lips. "I don't think we're going to be leaving this room before we land," I tease, my voice a mix of satisfaction and amusement.

Julie laughs, her eyes alive with a gleam of mischief. "Awfully sure of yourself, aren't you?"

I raise an eyebrow, intrigued by her playful challenge. "Are you going to tell me I'm wrong?"

She leans closer, her breath a warm whisper against my cheek. "Nope, not even close."

Pulling her into my arms, I nuzzle my face into her hair and breathe deeply.

We lay together in the quiet that follows, a tangle of limbs and contentment. It's not long before she drifts off to sleep, and I'm quick to follow her.

CHAPTER 15

JULIE

I find myself in the middle of a dream that feels both surreal and vividly real. My eyes flutter open, and I'm immediately struck by the unfamiliar yet beautiful surroundings. The room is lovely and spacious, bathed in soft light, every detail crisp and clean. The windows are wide open, letting in a gentle breeze that carries the fresh, salty scent of the ocean.

For a moment I just lie there, soaking in the peacefulness of the room. The bed is incredibly comfortable, the kind you sink into and never want to leave. But it's the sound of children laughing that eventually pulls me from the cocoon of the sheets. It's a sound full of joy and innocence, and it makes my heart feel lighter just hearing it.

I rise slowly, my feet touching the cool floor, and start to wander through the house. It's enormous, every inch of it exuding a sense of luxury and comfort. The kind of place I've seen in movies but never imagined I'd be in. The walls are adorned with art that's both intriguing and beautiful, and every window offers a breathtaking view of the endless ocean stretching out to the horizon.

I follow the sound of laughter, finding myself drawn to it like a moth to a flame. It leads me to the living room, a vast space with floor-to-ceiling windows that frame the stunning seascape outside.

There, in the middle of the room, are two beautiful children, their giggles filling the air. They're playing some sort of game, completely engrossed in their own little world. I can't see their faces, but there's something familiar about them, something that tugs at my heart.

There's a man sitting with them, his back to me, but there's a familiarity about him, as well. His posture, the way he interacts with the children, is undeniably captivating. Even from this angle, I can tell he's handsome, with broad shoulders and an air of gentle strength about him. The way the children gravitate toward him, their trust and love evident in their easy laughter, is heartwarming.

I stand there watching them, a sense of bliss enveloping me. It's a feeling I've never known before, a deep, fulfilling contentment that seems to seep into my very bones. This scene, this moment, it feels like everything I've ever wanted, everything I didn't know I was longing for.

But just as the man begins to turn around, just as I'm about to see his face, the dream starts to slip away. The edges of the room blur, the sound of the ocean fades, and the laughter becomes distant.

I awaken, the remnants of the dream still clinging to me, leaving a lingering sense of loss in its wake. I am still in the bedroom on the plane, familiar yet stark compared to the dream. The ocean is gone, replaced by the view of the rolling white clouds below.

I lie there for a moment, trying to hold onto the dream, to the feeling of utter happiness it brought me. But it's quickly slipping away, like sand through my fingers. All that remains is a sense of longing, a yearning for something I can't quite put my finger on.

I blink away the remnants of the dream, my eyes adjusting to the reality of my surroundings. Plush and luxurious, but a far cry from the fantasy I'd just woken from. As the memories of what happened with Ivan flood back, a warm flush spreads through me. The passion, the intensity of our encounter is still so vivid, so fresh in my mind.

For a brief moment, I entertain the thought of a round two but when I turn to the other side of the bed, expecting to find Ivan, I'm met with nothing but neatly tucked sheets and the cool absence of his presence.

He's gone, leaving behind only the memory of our heat.

I let out a sigh, a cocktail of disappointment and irritation bubbling up inside me. I shake my head, pushing back the sheets as I swing my legs over the side of the bed. Standing up, I stretch, feeling the pleasant soreness in my muscles, a physical reminder of our passionate escapade.

Stepping into the bathroom, I'm greeted by an opulence that matches the rest of the plane. The marble tiles are cool under my feet, and the fixtures gleam with a polished shine. It's like stepping into a spa, a private sanctuary in the sky.

Turning on the shower, I step under the warm spray, letting the water cascade over me. I close my eyes, letting my mind drift back to Ivan, to the way his hands felt on my skin, the way his lips moved against mine. Fantasies start to play out in my head, each scenario more tantalizing than the last.

Finally, I force myself to step out of the shower, reaching for a towel to dry off. My reflection in the mirror is a mix of flushed skin and tousled hair, the aftermath of an afternoon spent in the arms of a man who's as infuriating as he is irresistible.

As I wrap the towel around myself, a part of me is still irked with Ivan for disappearing. I can't say I'm surprised; he's all control and composure, even in the aftermath of passion. But another part of me, the part that's still riding the high of amazing sex, can't help but wonder what's next.

What does all of this mean for us? For me? The questions swirl in my head as I step out of the bathroom, ready to face whatever the rest of the day has in store. The adventure in Bora Bora awaits, and with it, the promise of more unexpected turns and hopefully, more moments of undeniable chemistry with my new husband.

Stepping out wrapped in the plush robe that awaited me, I can't help but feel a tad scandalous. The hem barely brushes mid-thigh, leaving a generous amount of leg on display. I catch a glimpse of the monogram JS elegantly stitched on the chest.

A smile tugs at my lips. Ivan's thoughtfulness is a sweet surprise, though I can't shake the suspicion that he might have had a secondary motive in choosing such a revealing robe.

I slip into the fuzzy slippers, their softness a welcome feeling on my feet. I'm feeling a bit like a sultry, yet cozy, version of Cinderella, as I make my way into the main cabin.

Ivan is engrossed in his laptop. He's like a statue, all chiseled lines and intense concentration.

"Working hard or hardly working, Mr. Stepanov?" I quip, leaning against the edge of the table, trying to draw his attention. "Aren't we supposed to be on our honeymoon?"

After a moment or two, he finally looks up, and his gaze immediately takes a leisurely stroll down the length of my robe-clad form. It's a look that sends a thrill of excitement through me, a reminder of the afternoon's passion. But there's a distraction in his eyes, a hint of preoccupation that tempers the heat in his gaze.

"We won't be landing for a few more hours," he says, his voice carrying his usual brand of efficiency. "I have some work that needs my attention. Feel free to entertain yourself with the television, or you could grab your laptop if you'd like."

I raise an eyebrow, my smile still in place. "Really, Ivan? Even thirty-thousand feet in the air, you can't take a break from being CEO?" I tease, trying to lighten the mood, to bring back that spark of connection.

He offers a small, apologetic smile, but it's clear his mind is elsewhere, tangled in the webs of business and responsibility. "Duty calls, Julie. Even in the skies."

I let out a mock sigh, my hand flitting to my hip in a playful gesture. "Well, if I must be left to my own devices, I suppose I'll just have to find a way to amuse myself. But don't work too hard. Remember, we're supposed to be celebrating."

Turning away, I head toward the plush seats, my mind already racing with possibilities. Television, maybe, or perhaps diving into a good book. There's a certain allure to having this time to myself, a chance to relax and unwind in the lap of luxury.

Still, there's a part of me that can't help but wish Ivan would close that laptop and join me, turn back into the man who kissed me so passionately just a few hours ago.

Landing on the couch with a huff, I can't shake off the feeling of being dismissed. It's absurd, really, feeling snubbed by a guy whose marriage proposal was nothing more than a business deal.

But emotions, much like the rich aroma of coffee wafting through the cabin of the plane, don't always follow logic. They linger, potent and undeniable.

Enough of this, I decide. *Time to shake things up a bit, Julie.* Rising from the couch, I saunter over to Ivan with purpose. He's still buried in his work, the very picture of corporate dedication.

Kneeling in front of him, I'm fully aware of how suggestive my position is, especially in this barely-there robe. I place my hand on his thigh, feeling his firm muscle beneath the fabric of his trousers. "So, Mr. Stepanov, are you planning to work the entire flight?" My voice drips with a playful challenge, my eyes locked on his.

Ivan's gaze drops to meet mine, and there's a flicker of something more than just professional interest in his eyes. It's a look that suggests he's considering all of the possibilities that could happen with me on my knees in front of him.

He reaches out, his fingers brushing my chin in a gentle caress that sends a shiver down my spine. "I need to work on the plane," he says, his voice low and resonant. "But once we reach the islands, I'll put it away. You have my word."

There's something in the way he says it—firm, yet tender—that makes me believe him. I lean in and press a quick, soft kiss to his lips, a promise of more to come. Rising, I straighten my robe, satisfied with the promise I was able to extract from him.

Ivan watches me, a hint of a smile playing at the corners of his mouth. "The flight attendants have laid out dinner for you, whenever you're ready," he says, turning back to his laptop.

Dinner for one. Not exactly the romantic honeymoon meal I might have imagined, but then again, this isn't exactly a traditional honeymoon. I head toward the dining area, the plush carpet beneath my feet.

As I sit down at the elegantly set table, I can't help but feel a twinge of loneliness. It's quiet, save for the soft hum of the engine and the occasional click of Ivan's keyboard. It's a far cry from the passion and connection we shared just hours ago.

Even still, I can't deny the thrill that pulses through me at the thought of what awaits us in Bora Bora. The promise of tropical beaches, endless blue skies, and perhaps a chance to explore this strange, new dynamic between us.

CHAPTER 16

JULIE

Touching down in Bora Bora, I'm braced for more Ivan-the-businessman, but as soon as he steps off the plane, it's apparent he's shed his corporate skin. Suddenly, he's Ivan-on-vacation, and it's a hell of a transformation.

Our seaside cottage is nothing short of a paradise retreat. Nestled away from the bustling resort, it's a private sanctuary where the only sounds are the gentle lapping of the ocean and the rustling of palm leaves in the breeze.

The interior is a vision, airy and open, with a bed that looks like it was made for royalty. The view of the ocean is so stunning it almost seems photoshopped, and every detail, from the soft linens to the tropical flowers on the table, whispers romance.

But the real magic happens on the beach. Ivan leads me to a private cabana, set up just for us, with curtains fluttering in the soft ocean breeze. It's secluded, romantic, and unbelievably sexy.

The heat isn't just from the sun. There's an undeniable flame between us, a sizzle that's been building since we boarded the plane, and clearly wasn't sated by our steamy encounter on the flight here.

Things escalate pretty quickly. The sun, the sea, the secluded cabana, it's like we're in our own little world. Ivan's touch is electric, his kisses deep and passionate. When he pulls me close, the feel of his body against mine is enough to make me forget this is barely more than a contractual obligation.

We make love with the curtains billowing around us, the gentle ocean breeze mingling with the heat of our bodies. It's passionate, intense, and surprisingly tender. Ivan, the stoic, always-in-control CEO, shows a side of him I've never seen before—caring, attentive, and dare I say, a little playful.

As we lay there afterward, listening to the waves and feeling the warm breeze on our skin, I can't help but wonder if this tender side of him is just a vacation thing or if there's more to it. Ivan is much different here, away from the office and the pressures of his corporate world. He's more relaxed, more open, and incredibly charming.

But as the sun sets, painting the sky in shades of orange and pink, I remind myself to keep my guard up. This is still Ivan Stepanov and this arrangement is as unconventional as it gets. I'm here to enjoy the moment, the luxury, the sex, but I'm not about to lose myself in a fantasy that's just going to dissipate as soon as we return home.

The second day on the island ushers in a new adventure, and it's like stepping into a glossy travel brochure. Ivan has arranged a private lagoon cruise on a boat that's more like a floating palace. The deck gleams under the sun, the white sails billow like clouds in the clear blue sky, and I'm pretty sure the sea is showing off just for us—sparkling turquoise water inviting us in.

As we set sail, the breeze tousles my hair, and I can't help but feel like I'm in some kind of dream. Ivan stands beside me, his hand holding mine, his touch grounding me in this surreal moment. He's got an interesting look in his eye, a combination of excitement and a promise of more than just scenic views.

We arrive at the reef to go scuba diving and I'm all suited up, feeling a bit like an astronaut about to step onto an alien planet. The ocean below us is a mystery, a world I've only ever glimpsed through the glass at the New York Aquarium. But with Ivan by my side, guiding me and encouraging me, I'm ready to dive in.

The water is crystal clear, a window into a world of vibrant colors and animated life. We're greeted by sea turtles that glide past with a grace that's almost otherworldly. There are so many fish in colors so bright and patterns so intricate, I feel like I'm swimming in a living, breathing masterpiece.

But amidst this incredible experience and all of these amazing views, it's Ivan who's the real surprise. He's become a completely different person since we arrived here. He's relaxed and playful, vulnerable and romantic. He holds my hand as we watch the sea turtles, sneaking kisses under the water that leave me giggling into my snorkel. He whispers naughty promises in my ear, his voice low and husky, causing my insides to quiver.

It's in these moments of stolen kisses and whispered promises that really get to me. Ivan is slowly weaving his way into my heart. He's showing me a side of him I never knew existed—a man who can laugh and be tender, one who can look at me like I'm the only woman in the world.

I came to Bora Bora expecting a luxurious vacation with my businessman husband. What I didn't expect was to find a connection, a chemistry going beyond convenience and contracts. Ivan is slowly revealing himself to be so much more.

We're like a couple of teenagers, unable to keep our hands off each other. We make love two, three times a day, and each time is like the first, filled with a hunger and urgency that leaves me breathless. He's opened a door to a part of me I didn't even know existed.

Every touch, every kiss, is a discovery, a revelation of pleasure and connection.

But it's not just the physical aspect. Ivan is making me feel things I didn't want to feel, things I didn't think were possible to feel in our arrangement. He's tender, attentive, and when he looks at me, it's like he's seeing right into my soul. It's both exhilarating and terrifying.

After a few days in paradise, business creeps up on us that Ivan has to attend to. I can't help but feel a twinge of disappointment.

"I seem to remember you making a promise to put work away while we were here," I say, a weak smile on my face that suggests I'm only half-joking.

Part of me expects him to dismiss my concerns. Ivan's the kind of man for whom work always comes first. Instead, he looks genuinely frustrated with himself. He steps over to me and places his hand on my shoulder. To my surprise, his touch calms me instantly.

"I know. And I never want to be the sort of husband who breaks promises." He glances away thoughtfully before speaking again. "How about this—give me a bit of time to wrap up these work matters, and I'll make myself unavailable for the rest of the trip. I'll set up automatic replies for my email and phone stating I'm out of the office."

There's no doubt in my mind that he's being sincere with what he's saying.

"That would be nice," I say. "It really would."

"Head into town and do a little shopping therapy. I'll text you when I'm all done."

But the idea of wandering around souvenir stores doesn't appeal to me. Instead, I opt for something more low-key.

"I think I'll just wander down the beach," I tell him. "Maybe find a good book in the gift shop at the nearby resort."

He kisses my forehead and gives my hand a squeeze. I feel a pang of longing as he pulls away. "Enjoy your day," he says, his voice carrying a note of regret.

After he leaves, I'm struck by the sudden silence, the absence of his presence. The cottage feels too big, too empty without him. I shake off the feeling, telling myself this is just a temporary thing, a fun interlude in an otherwise practical arrangement.

The ocean stretches out before me in endless shades of blue. The breeze plays with my hair, and I take a deep breath, filling my lungs with the salty air. This is my time to relax, to soak in the beauty of this place.

But as I walk, my mind drifts back to Ivan, to the moments we've shared. I'm experiencing a confusing mix of emotions; the joy of newfound passion, the uncertainty of what it all means, the reality of our circumstances. I came here as his wife in name only, but now, I'm not so sure what I am.

The nearby resort's main building looms ahead. As I enter the cool, air-conditioned lobby, I head straight for the gift shop. I peruse the many beautiful items before heading over to the book section, choosing a best seller with reviews that assure me it's a great 'beach read.'

I find a quiet spot on the beach, the waves lapping gently at the shore. Settling down, I open the book and let my thoughts wander, the sound of the ocean a soothing backdrop to my reflections.

I begin to read but my mind is far from relaxed. I can't help but wonder about Ivan's intentions. Is this week in paradise a glimpse into a future filled with romance and passion, or is it just a temporary escape from reality, a brief interlude in an otherwise transactional relationship?

His behavior this week has been anything but businesslike. The way he looks at me, touches me, kisses me, it's as if he's truly present, truly with me as my husband. But when business calls, he slips back into the world of deals and decisions, leaving me adrift in a sea of uncertainty.

And what about the future? The child we've agreed to have —will he be as attentive and caring with our baby as he's been with me this week? I stopped taking my birth control the day I signed the prenup, as we agreed. It's a commitment, a step toward something real and lasting. But can I trust that he'll be there, not just physically, but emotionally too?

I shake my head, trying to dispel the doubts. I'm reading too much into this, overthinking things. I know Ivan; I've seen how he operates. He's a workaholic but he's also shown a side of himself that's kind, romantic, and seemingly genuine in his desire for a child. I can't imagine him being anything but a devoted father.

Still, the nagging doubts linger. What happens when we return home? Will we slip back into our roles of CEO and assistant, even though he said that I would no longer be working as his PA? Will the passion and connection of the tropics fade like a dream upon waking?

I chastise myself for the pessimistic thoughts. I need to enjoy every moment in this incredible place, savor the now. Worrying about the future, about what might or might not happen, is a surefire way to spoil the present.

I make a conscious decision to push aside my worries. I'm in a tropical paradise, with a man who, for all his complexities, has shown me a world of pleasure and affection I never knew existed.

I'm determined to enjoy it while it lasts.

I focus back on the book, settling in for a quiet, relaxing afternoon.

CHAPTER 17

IVAN

The boardwalk beneath my feet is a familiar path now, leading back to the private cottage where Julie waits.

The sun is setting, casting a golden hue over the ocean, a picturesque scene that belies the turmoil in my mind. Julie's disappointment earlier was palpable, a silent accusation that I'm not fully present, not fully committed to this honeymoon of ours.

I made plans for tomorrow to make up for today's absence. I have arranged for activities that I know will delight Julie; experiences designed to create memories we'll both cherish. Yet as I make my way back, a nagging unease settles over me.

The sound of voices behind me pulls me from my thoughts. I slow my pace, my senses heightened. The voices are masculine, carrying a tone that doesn't quite fit the serene surroundings. I turn, my gaze landing on two men dressed in boating attire.

They don't look like typical tourists or locals. There's a certain alertness in their posture, a readiness that's out of place in this relaxed setting. My instincts—honed from years in a world where trust is a luxury and danger often lurks in the shadows—kick in. I assess them quickly, noting their build, the way they carry themselves, the way they scan their surroundings.

Our cottage is secluded, the last one on this stretch of the boardwalk. The presence of these men is no coincidence. I feel a surge of protectiveness, an instinctive need to get to Julie as quickly as I can.

As they continue to approach, my body tenses, ready for a confrontation. Every scenario runs through my mind, each one ending with me ensuring Julie's safety. However, just as I'm preparing to confront them, to demand what business they have, they veer off the path, disappearing down a narrow trail marked 'Employees Only.'

I watch them go; my suspicion not entirely abated. Their sudden change of direction does little to convince me of their innocence. I make a mental note of their appearance and the direction they took.

In my world, caution is always warranted, and I can't afford to let my guard down, not even in paradise.

As I stride onto the deck of the cottage I notice Julie, completely absorbed in her book. The title catches my eye: 'Tangled Hearts.' It appears to be a light, fun romance novel, the kind that promises escapism and a touch of whimsy. I can't help but smile at her choice, so different from the business and strategy books that fill my own shelves.

I clear my throat lightly and Julie looks up, her expression shifting from the dreamy haze of the book's contents to the present moment. "Enjoying your read?" I ask, a teasing note in my voice.

She grins, closing the book and setting it aside. "Oh, absolutely. Nothing like a good romance to distract you on a lazy beach day," she replies, her tone playful.

I lean against the railing, watching her. "I must admit, I've never understood the appeal of those kinds of books. Don't they all have the same plot?" I ask, genuinely curious.

Julie laughs, a light, carefree sound. "Maybe, but it's all about the journey, not the destination. Besides, who doesn't want a little love story now and then?" she retorts, her eyes sparkling with delight.

I nod, considering her words. "Perhaps I've been missing out. Maybe you can recommend a good one for me. Something to broaden my horizons beyond corporate strategies and market analyses."

She tilts her head, appraising me with a hint of mischief. "I'll have to think about that. But be warned, it might flip your world upside down when it comes to love."

The smile that spreads across her face is one of genuine warmth, a contrast to the composed, professional demeanor I'm used to. It's a smile that reaches her eyes, transforming her entire expression, and for a moment, I'm caught off guard by the rush of emotion it stirs within me.

My heart, usually so guarded, so carefully shielded, falters as a realization hits me with unexpected force. The barriers I've erected, the rules I've set to keep emotions at bay are wavering in the face of this woman. What began as a convenient solution, a means to an end, is quickly becoming something more, something dangerously close to genuine affection.

"Have you learned anything useful in your book?" I ask. I'm curious to see how she'll respond, knowing full well the steamy nature of such reads.

She looks up, a sly grin spreading across her face. Her eyes sparkle with mischief and she winks, fully understanding the implication behind my question.

"Oh, maybe a thing or two," she replies, her tone playful yet suggestive.

She sets the book aside and stands up, her movements fluid and inviting. "Why don't you come over here and I'll show you?"

I can't resist her invitation.

Without another word, I close the distance between us, my resolve to maintain a professional distance crumbling under the weight of this newfound realization. I lean down, capturing her lips in a kiss that's meant to be brief, a simple gesture of affection.

But the moment our lips meet it morphs into more, a kiss that's deep, intense, and unexpectedly revealing.

The exchange leaves us both breathless, a silent acknowledgment of the burgeoning connection between us. "Dinner will be delivered soon," I manage to say, my voice a little rougher than intended.

Her response catches me off guard. "I'm only hungry for one thing," she says, her voice a sultry whisper that immediately turns my cock to stone.

Our lips meet again in a dance of passion, exploring and tasting, each kiss deepening the bond that's been simmering beneath the surface. We slip out of our clothing with an ease that speaks of our growing comfort with each other, our banter playful yet laced with an undercurrent of a longing desire.

The air around us is charged with electricity, every touch sending sparks through my veins. I guide her toward the bedroom, my hand firmly yet gently on her lower back.

Once inside, the soft light casts a warm glow over us, creating an ambiance of sensuality and anticipation. I pause for a moment, gazing into her eyes, gauging her readiness for what I'm about to propose.

"Julie," I begin, my voice low and steady, "have you ever explored the dynamics of domination and submission?" My question hangs in the air, an invitation to a world of heightened sensations and trust.

She looks at me, her eyes wide with curiosity. "No, I haven't," she admits, her voice tinged with a hint of excitement. "But I'm always open to new experiences."

I nod, pleased with her willingness to explore. "It's about trust and surrender. About giving and taking control in a way that heightens every sensation, every emotion."

I step closer to her, my presence commanding yet reassuring. "I'll lead, and you'll follow. You can stop at any time, just say the word. But if you'll trust me, I can show you pleasures you've never imagined."

Her breath quickens, and I can see the anticipation building in her eyes. She nods, a silent agreement to my promise.

I begin to guide her with a calm yet authoritative presence. "Stand here," I instruct, pointing to a spot just in front of me. "Face me."

She does as directed, her movements graceful yet tinged with a hint of nervous anticipation. Her eyes meet mine, searching for reassurance, and I offer her a small, encouraging smile.

"Now," I continue, my voice low and steady, "I want you to close your eyes. Just focus on my voice and let yourself feel."

She complies, her eyelids fluttering shut, and I watch as a sense of trust washes over her features. "Good," I praise gently. "Now relax. Feel the space around you. Feel my presence."

I step closer, my breath mingling with hers. "I'm going to touch your arm now," I say, ensuring she's prepared for each interaction. As my fingers trail softly up her arm, I feel her shiver slightly at the contact.

"How does that feel?" I ask, my voice a whisper.

"It's good," she replies, a tremor in her voice revealing her growing arousal.

"Remember, if you want to stop, just say so. You're in control, even when surrendering to me," I remind her, emphasizing the importance of her consent and comfort.

I guide her through a series of simple, yet intimate commands, each designed to heighten her awareness and response to my touch. "Turn around, slowly," I instruct. "Feel each movement, each moment."

As she turns, I continue to guide her with my voice. "Now, lean back against me. Let yourself feel supported, safe."

She leans back, her body pressing lightly against mine, and I sense her easing into the experience, her initial tension melting away under my guidance.

"Trust me, Julie. Let go. Feel the freedom in surrender," I whisper into her ear, my hands resting lightly on her hips.

As she leans back, trusting me, I gently guide her arms behind her back. "I'm going to bind your wrists. It's all part of the experience, the trust," I explain softly, my voice a steady presence as I secure her hands with a soft, silken rope. The binding is firm but gentle.

Her breath hitches slightly at the sensation, a mix of anticipation and exhilaration evident in her posture, her back arching. "How does that feel?" I ask, ensuring her comfort is paramount.

"It's different, but exciting," she admits, a tremor in her voice betraying her growing eagerness.

I move closer to her, my body barely grazing hers, my breath warm against her neck. "Focus on the sensations. Let yourself be present in this moment, in every touch," I guide her, my hands tracing over her bound wrists, up her arms, and along the contours of her body.

Her breathing becomes more labored, a clear sign of her rising arousal. The restriction of movement seems to amplify her senses, each touch magnified, each caress sending waves of anticipation through her.

"You're doing great," I encourage her, my voice low and seductive.

As I continue to explore her body, her responses become more fervent, her body arching instinctively toward my touch. The combination of restraint and stimulation is weaving a potent spell, drawing her deeper into the experience.

"You're so responsive, Julie. So beautifully responsive," I murmur, watching as she writhes gently, bound yet free.

I can feel her body responding, the tension building like a crescendo. "Focus on my touch, on the sensations," I guide her, my words as much a caress as my fingers.

My finger trails down her front, along the flat plane of her stomach, over the thatch of hair above her pussy. She moans and squirms against me. Soon I'm right above her womanhood, my touch teasing her. She's yearning, pressing her body against mine, guiding me without words.

I decide that the teasing has gone on for long enough. I move my hand between the warm silkiness of her thighs and guide her to spread them. She does, and I wrap my arm around her middle to hold her in place as I spread her lips open.

"Yes... yes, just like that." Her words come out in pants, her breasts rising and falling as I tease her clit with my thumb. She's soaking wet, letting me know in the most direct way how she's feeling about our little experiment in pleasure.

I enter her with a pair of fingers. She moans again, clenching around my touch, bucking her hips into my hand. She's warm and wet as I move in and out of her, her breaths coming quicker and quicker.

"Are you going to come for me?" I ask.

"Yes. I'm so damn close."

I smirk. "Good. But you're not going to do so until I tell you. Understood?"

"Y-yes."

"Excellent."

I continue to touch her, quickening and slowing my pace, bringing her to the edge only to pull her right back. Her legs are starting to shake, and I get the distinct impression that, without my holding her up, Julie would've collapsed under my touch.

Finally, I decide it's time.

"Now. Come for me."

Her hands clench and unclench, a physical manifestation of her internal struggle between control and surrender. "Ivan..." she gasps, her voice trembling.

"That's it, Julie. Let go," I coax, my touch becoming more focused, more purposeful as I guide her toward release.

As she nears the brink, her body tenses, a bowstring pulled taut. "You're almost there," I whisper, my voice a steady anchor in the storm of her sensations. "Let it happen."

With a final, gentle push from my fingers, she crosses the threshold, her body shuddering with release. "Ivan!" she cries out, her voice a raw, beautiful sound that fills the room.

I pull her gently into my arms, holding her as she comes down from the climax, her body still quivering with aftershocks. "You were incredible," I tell her, my voice filled with genuine admiration and a hint of awe at her trust and openness.

But we're not done yet.

CHAPTER 18

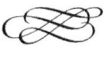

JULIE

I'm standing bound and blissfully lost in a haze of desire, my eyes drinking in the sight of Ivan standing before me, a vision of masculine power and allure.

Panting slightly, I manage to find my voice. "What's next?" I ask, my words laced with a mix of anticipation and a hint of daring. I'm new to this game, but there's an excitement brewing within me, a curiosity to explore these uncharted waters.

Ivan's eyes lock onto mine, a spark of something indefinable flickering in their depths. "Remember the plane? When you were on your knees in front of me?" His voice is a low growl, sending shivers down my spine.

I nod, a slow smile spreading across my face as I recall the moment.

He steps closer, the air around us charged with a heady mix of anticipation and desire. "I want you to continue what you started. Show me what you can do," he commands, his tone firm, laced with an undercurrent of longing.

"Going to be a little hard with my hands tied behind me," I say, tilting my head back toward the bindings.

I expect him to release me. But he only grins.

"Be creative."

I sink to my knees in front of him as he sits on the edge of the bed.

I lean forward, taking the waistband of his underwear in my teeth and tugging them down. It takes a little doing and a bit of his help, but I'm able to peel them down along his powerful thighs, his cock springing out to greet me.

"There you go," he says approvingly.

He stands so I can pull them down the rest of the way and steps out of them. I sit up, his glorious, perfect cock my reward, the end glistening with a dab of precum, a signal he's just as turned on as I am.

"Now," he says. "Show me what you can do."

I lean forward, flicking his head with my tongue.

"How do I taste?" he asks.

"Delicious."

He's long and thick, and for a moment I find myself wondering how the hell I'm supposed to do this without the use of my hands. Finally, I lean forward, kissing his tip, opening my mouth and taking him inside. He's warm and hard, the taste of him a perfect blend of sweet and salty, washing over my palate.

It's difficult with no hands. My instinct is to take hold of his length, stroking it as I suck. But I have to do all the work with nothing more than my lips and tongue. It's a bit awkward at first, but soon I feel like I'm in my element.

My lips go up and down his shaft as I take as much of him into my mouth as possible. His groans, the way he brushes my hair aside to get a better look, encourage me. His massive cock strains my jaw a bit, so I take breaks to lick him up and down.

Just as he's about to cross the threshold, he gently but firmly guides me up to a standing position.

"Julie," Ivan's voice is firm, "I want you to get on the bed. On all fours." He reaches behind me and quickly tugs my bindings free.

I feel a flush of heat spread across my cheeks, my heart pounding with each step toward the bed.

I pause for a moment, glancing back at Ivan. His eyes are dark with longing, a silent encouragement for me to proceed.

As I position myself on the bed, the coolness of the sheets contrasts sharply with the warmth of my skin. I'm acutely aware of every sensation, every breath, as I wait for Ivan's next command, the air thick with expectation.

The thrill of surrendering to him, of giving him complete control, is both intimidating and exhilarating.

Positioned as he directed, I feel exposed yet empowered, a paradox of sensations that only heightens my arousal. Ivan's approach is deliberate. I can sense his gaze on me, appraising, calculating, igniting a fire within that I didn't know could burn so fiercely.

His hands find me, strong and insistent. As he enters me, the connection is immediate and overwhelming, a fusion of physical pleasure and emotional intensity that consumes me.

Ivan's voice is both commanding and reassuring as he guides me. "That's it," he says, his tone firm but encouraging. "Just relax and let yourself feel everything."

I nod slightly, my body responding to his words, the tension slowly ebbing away under his guidance. His hands are gentle yet assertive on my skin, directing me, pushing me further into this new realm of sensation. His touch moves along the curves of my hip, all the way to my breasts as they sway back and forth with each full, deep thrust.

When I feel like I can't take any more, when the need within me is a roaring blaze, he gives the command I've been waiting for. "Finish," he says, his voice a deep growl that resonates with my own need.

The release, when it comes, is explosive, a culmination of all the pent-up desire and tension. We reach our climax together, a symphony of shared pleasure that echoes through the room. It's a moment of perfect synchronicity, his cock pulsing and erupting inside of me as my own orgasm rips through my body, my limbs shaking with pleasure and causing me to fall forward, his manhood still buried inside of me.

We collapse together, spent and satisfied. Lying there in the afterglow, the room is filled with a content energy. The gentle caress of Ivan's hand on my skin is soothing. Our fingers entwine, and I feel a connection that goes beyond the physical, a sense of being understood and cherished.

Without thinking, I find myself curling into him, seeking the warmth and protection of his embrace. His arm wraps around me, strong and secure, pulling me closer. It's a gesture that speaks volumes, conveying a sense of safety and belonging that I've longed for but never quite found.

As sleep begins to claim me, I feel a profound gratitude for this moment, for the unexpected journey that's brought me here.

I let out a contented sigh, my last conscious thought a reflection of how much my life has changed since meeting Ivan. From the structured, predictable routine of my days as his assistant to the passionate, unpredictable reality of being his wife, it's been a journey of discovery and growth.

As I drift off to sleep in the warmth of his embrace, lulled by the sound of the ocean and the steady beat of his heart, I can't help but feel a sense of excitement for the future.

It's a future that's uncertain, filled with potential challenges and unknowns, but also with the possibility of love, connection, and a shared life that's richer and more fulfilling than anything I could have imagined.

CHAPTER 19

IVAN

As the sun rises on our last day in Bora Bora, I'm acutely aware of the ticking clock, the inevitable return to reality looming over us. I'm determined to make every moment count, to create memories with Julie that will transcend the boundaries of this idyllic escape.

We start our day with an early morning swim in the crystal-clear lagoon, the water like liquid glass around us. Julie's laughter echoes as we race each other to a small, uninhabited island a short distance from the shore. Her competitive spirit is infectious, and I find myself admiring her determination and zest for life.

After our swim, we enjoy a relaxing breakfast on the beach, the sand cool beneath our feet, the air filled with the scent of tropical flowers and fresh fruit. We talk about everything and nothing, our conversation flowing as easily as the gentle breeze around us.

In the afternoon, we take a hike through the lush tropical forest, the canopy above us alive with the sounds of exotic birds and rustling leaves. The trail leads us to a hidden waterfall, its waters cascading into a natural pool. We swim in the cool, refreshing water, the sense of seclusion and tranquility enveloping us.

In the evening, we have our final meal at the nearby resort. The ambiance of the space is impeccable, a perfect blend of luxury and elegance, the view a full sweep of the sun setting over the western waters, the sky alight with reds and oranges.

Yet amidst the splendor, the real view that captures my attention, the sight that sets my pulse racing, is Julie. She looks absolutely radiant, wearing a dress that seems to have been crafted just for her.

It's a deep, rich blue, a color that compliments her eyes and makes her skin glow under the soft lighting of the restaurant. The fabric hugs her curves in a way that's both elegant and tantalizing, accentuating her figure with a grace and sensuality that's impossible to ignore.

Finally, as we're enjoying the delicious flavors of our third course, I find the courage to broach the subject. "Julie," I begin, pausing to choose my words carefully. "I've been thinking about our return to the office. Would you be willing to continue working as my assistant for the time being and train your successor once I find someone suitable?"

She looks up from her plate, a flicker of surprise in her eyes, which quickly turns into amusement. A soft laugh escapes her lips, the sound as delightful as the music playing softly in the background. "Of course," she replies, her eyes sparkling with a mixture of humor and sincerity. "I wouldn't dream of leaving you in a crunch."

Relief washes over me, but before I can express my gratitude, she adds with a playful tilt of her head, "But, you know, if you want to keep any assistant, you might have to work on being a bit nicer. They won't all be as tolerant as I am."

I can't help but smile at her comment, recognizing the truth in her words. "I'll take that under advisement," I say, my tone light but acknowledging the validity of her suggestion.

"I'm serious," she says, leaning forward. "You're going to have to learn to be a little bit less of a grumpy old man."

"An old man, huh?" I reply, my voice low and teasing. "I think I'll have to show you just how wrong you are about that."

The moment is charged with an undeniable heat, a current of electricity that runs between us, only to be interrupted by the waiter arriving with our main course.

Another matter comes to mind as we dig in. "Have you given any thought to what you'll do with your apartment now?" I ask, my tone shifting to something more serious.

She pauses, a frown creasing her brow as she contemplates the question. "You know, I hadn't really thought about giving it up," she admits, a hint of surprise in her voice. "It's strange to think about moving out of my place."

Her frown shifts to a laugh, light and carefree. "It's funny, isn't it? We're married, and I've never even been to your home." Her eyes meet mine, sparkling with amusement and a touch of curiosity.

I chuckle in response, recognizing the absurdity of the situation. "It is rather unusual, I suppose. But then, our entire arrangement has been anything but conventional," I say, my gaze holding hers.

"We should rectify that soon," I add, a genuine smile playing on my lips. "You should come see where you'll be living, get a feel for the place. It's quite different from your apartment, I can assure you."

Julie nods, her eyes alight with interest. "I'd like that. It'll be a big change, but I'm starting to think that change can be a good thing."

"My place is quite plain," I admit, stirring my wine glass idly. "I've never been one for decorating. But as my wife, you're welcome to add your own touch, make it more homey."

Julie's eyes light up, sparkling with an enthusiasm that I find both endearing and unexpected. "Really? I get to decorate?" she asks, her voice tinged with excitement. "I can't wait to see it, to get an idea of what you already have and what I can add."

Her excitement is contagious, her words spilling out in a continuous stream of ideas and possibilities. I watch her, silently captivated by the vibrancy she exudes. It's a side of her I haven't seen before, one that's full of life and creativity.

I remain outwardly composed, my expression betraying none of the effect she's having on me. Yet inwardly, I'm struck by the beauty of her enthusiasm, the way it transforms her, bringing a new dimension to her personality.

It is both alarming and encouraging. I've always been in control, always had a plan. But with Julie, it's different. She's bringing something new into my life, something unexpected and, perhaps, something necessary.

The realization that I might be falling for her, that love could be part of our equation, is a revelation. It's a concept I'd dismissed, but now, in the light of her joy and the connection we're building, it seems not only possible, but inevitable.

The night culminates in a passionate encounter that eclipses all others we've shared. In the privacy of our cottage, with the ocean as our soundtrack, we explore each other with an intense and fiery fervor. It's a connection that's physical, emotional, and deeply intimate, a dance of desire and affection that leaves us both breathless and sated.

But as we lie there in the afterglow, the reality of our impending departure casts a shadow over the moment. I find myself wondering how our relationship will fare once we're back in the world we left behind. The ease and freedom we've found here, will it survive the pressures and expectations of our everyday lives?

It's a dynamic that's bound to be fraught with challenges and complexities. But as I look at Julie, sleeping peacefully in my arms, I can't help but feel a sense of hope. Maybe what we've built here can withstand the trials of the real world. Maybe, against all odds, we can find a way to make this work.

I hold Julie close, feeling a sense of protectiveness and affection that's new and somewhat unsettling. This arrangement, which started as a practical solution, has evolved into something so much more, something I hadn't anticipated.

As we prepare to leave this paradise behind, I'm faced with the realization that what we've started here is only the beginning.

CHAPTER 20

JULIE

My jaw nearly hits the floor as the car pulls up in front of the Upper West Side brownstone Ivan calls home.

This place isn't just a house; it's a freaking monument. The classic brownstone facade is impeccably maintained, with ivy trailing up the sides, giving it an old-world charm that's rare in the city. It's like something out of a movie.

Ivan leads me inside, and I'm instantly struck by the sheer size of the place. The entryway alone could fit my entire apartment. High ceilings, polished hardwood floors, and an elegant staircase that spirals upward greet me. It's all so grand, I half-expect a butler to appear and take my coat.

But as we walk through the rooms, something odd catches my attention. Most of them are empty. No furniture, no artwork, nothing. The living room is a wide, open area with large windows that flood the space with light, but there's not a single couch or coffee table in sight.

I turn to Ivan, unable to hide my confusion. "So, uh, where's all your stuff?" I ask, gesturing to the barren room.

He shrugs, a faint smile playing on his lips. "I only use the bedroom, office, and kitchen. Never saw the point in filling up the rest."

I blink, trying to process this. Here's a man with one of the most beautiful homes I've ever seen, and he's living in it like it's a bachelor pad, less than a bachelor pad, actually. "Ivan, this place has so much potential! It's like a blank canvas begging for an artist."

He laughs at my dramatics, clearly amused by my horror. "Well, if you're so keen on it, I have something that might interest you." He fishes a credit card out of his pocket and hands it to me. It has my name on it.

"This is for you," he says. "There's a bank account set up in your name. Go wild with the furniture shopping. Turn this into a home you'll be comfortable in."

For a moment, I'm speechless, the card heavy in my hand. Then, a grin spreads across my face. I start walking through the rooms again, this time with a new sense of purpose. I can already picture a plush sofa here, a stylish coffee table there, maybe some modern art on the walls.

"This could be fun," I admit, excitement bubbling up inside me. "I get to decorate your house?"

He nods, watching me with an indulgent look. "Our house," he corrects gently. "And yes, decorate to your heart's content."

The word 'our' sends a warm tingle through me. Our house. It's a strange and thrilling thought. I spin around in the empty living room, my mind racing with ideas. "Well, prepare to be amazed. I've got some serious Pinterest boards to consult."

Ivan chuckles, his eyes following me as I dart from one room to another, the wheels spinning in my head. "I have no doubt," he says, leaning against the doorway. "Just promise me one thing."

I pause, looking back at him. "What's that?"

He smirks, a playful glint in his eye. "Try to leave at least one room set aside. For activities."

I laugh, shaking my head at his cheekiness. "You're incorrigible."

He steps closer, his presence suddenly filling the room. "But you like it," he speaks, his voice low.

I can't argue with that. Stepping into his arms, I tilt my head up to meet his kiss. The house, the future, the possibilities, all of it fades into the background as we lose ourselves in each other, right there in the middle of our big, empty living room that's just waiting to be filled with life.

Two weeks pass in a whirlwind of activity, and Ivan's once-empty house is transformed into a warm, inviting home. The living room now boasts a large comfy sectional sofa in a soft cream color, accented with vibrant throw pillows. A sleek, modern coffee table sits in the center, surrounded by lush indoor plants that bring a touch of nature inside. Abstract art adorns the walls, adding splashes of color and personality to the space.

The dining room is equally transformed, with a long, elegant table made of dark wood, surrounded by high-back chairs upholstered in a rich, royal blue. Above the table hangs a statement chandelier that casts a warm, inviting glow over the room.

In the kitchen, I've added small touches that make it feel more lived-in—a bowl of fresh fruit on the marble countertop, a set of stylish canisters for coffee and tea, and a couple of cookbooks displayed on a stand.

Ivan walks through the house, taking in all the changes. His initial hesitation has given way to genuine appreciation. "You've done a remarkable job, Julie," he says, his eyes scanning the place. "It feels like a home now."

I beam with pride, pleased with his reaction. "I'm glad you like it. It's been fun adding a bit of... well, me, to the place."

He nods, a smile tugging at his lips. " You've managed to make this place warm and inviting. It's a pleasant change."

Our relationship has undergone its own transformation, as well. Mutual respect and attraction have blossomed into something deeper, something that feels a lot like the beginnings of real affection. Yet, there's a part of Ivan that's holding back, focusing more on the physical aspect of our connection.

At work the next day, the reality of our professional relationship comes back into focus. Ivan has scheduled interviews for a new assistant, and while I know it's part of our agreement, I can't help feeling a twinge of reluctance at the thought of leaving my position.

In his office, Ivan looks over the resumes with a furrowed brow. "I've got three interviews lined up today," he says, sounding less than enthused. "But honestly, none of them seem quite right."

I lean against the doorframe, watching him. "You never know, one of them might surprise you."

He glances up, meeting my eyes. "I made you a promise to find a replacement. And I intend to keep it. But" he pauses, a hint of something unexpressed in his gaze, "I've grown accustomed to having you around. More than accustomed, actually."

I smile, a warm feeling spreading through me. "Well, whoever you hire will have big shoes to fill. But I'm not going anywhere just yet. I'll make sure they're up to speed before I step back."

Ivan nods, a look of gratitude in his eyes. "Thank you, Julie. That means a lot."

The air between us goes silent with unspoken words, a shared understanding of the unique dynamic we've built. As I turn to leave, Ivan calls out, "Julie?"

I look back, waiting.

He stands, crossing the room and stopping in front of me. "I just wanted to say I'm glad you're here. In every sense."

The sincerity in his voice catches me off guard, and for a moment, I'm speechless. Then, with a playful smile I reply, "Well, get used to it. I'm not going anywhere."

CHAPTER 21

IVAN

Checking my watch, I note there's some time before the interviews begin. On a whim, I decide to ask Julie to lunch. It's a small break from routine, but these small changes are bringing unexpected happiness.

I find her at her desk, absorbed in paperwork. "Julie," I say, leaning casually against the doorway, "how about joining me for lunch?"

She looks up, feigned surprise on her face as she rises. "Ivan Stepanov taking a lunch break instead of wolfing down a sandwich at his laptop? That's a first."

Julie picks a deli with a charming patio, a spot that exudes a relaxed atmosphere, a stark contrast to the usual stiff, formal dining settings I'm accustomed to. We settle at a table under an umbrella, the hum of the city around us a pleasant backdrop. She orders for both of us, her choices reflecting a casual ease I find refreshing.

As we wait for our food, Julie pulls out files from her bag, her efficiency on full display.

"Alright, let's see who we have lined up for today," she begins, her tone business-like but with an underlying warmth. "First, we have Martin Anders. He's got a solid background in corporate management, worked with some big names. Impressive on paper, but I have a feeling he might be a bit too assertive for your taste."

I lean back, listening, watching her. She knows me well, perhaps too well. The way she can predict my reactions, understand my preferences, is almost uncanny.

"Next is Eliza Graham. She's younger, less experienced, but very eager. Graduated top of her class, has a knack for languages. Might be a good fit if you're looking for fresh ideas," she continues, her finger tracing the lines of text.

"Languages, you say?" I murmur, intrigued. "That could be useful, considering our expanding international dealings."

Julie nods, her eyes meeting mine. "Exactly. She could bring a new perspective to the team. Plus, her references are glowing."

I can't help but smile at her thoroughness. Julie has always had a keen eye for talent, an ability to see potential where others might not.

"And the last one?" I ask, sipping my coffee.

"Ah, yes. Jonathan Kline. He's a bit of an enigma. Worked in various sectors, a bit of a jack-of-all-trades. Could be a wildcard, but sometimes that's exactly what you need."

Her analysis is spot-on, as usual. She has a way of cutting through the fluff, getting straight to the heart of the matter. It's one of the many reasons she's been more than just an assistant to me.

While she talks, I scan our surroundings. That's when I spot them—a pair of men seated a few tables behind us. One of them is too familiar for my liking. Our eyes meet, and he gives a subtle chin lift, a silent command for me to come over.

A surge of anger courses through me. No one summons Ivan Stepanov. But I can't afford to have a confrontation here, not in front of Julie. I need to handle this discreetly.

"I need to take care of something quickly," I say, my tone calm but firm. "I'll be right back."

She looks up, a flicker of concern crossing her features. "Is everything okay?"

"It's just a minor business matter," I assure her, though my mind is already racing with possibilities. There's no doubt that Boris has something to do with the presence of these men. They're goons, the sort of heavy-hitters you dispatch when you want to send a message of intimidation.

Standing up, I walk toward the men, my steps measured, my expression controlled. Their eyes are on me as I approach, evaluating, calculating. The familiar man smirks, a hint of smugness in his demeanor. I'm already formulating strategies, preparing for whatever this encounter might bring.

As I get closer, my gaze hardens. The recognition is instant. It's Karl, an associate from a past I'd rather forget. His companion, a stocky man with a brutish demeanor, eyes me with a mix of curiosity and challenge.

"What do you want, Karl?" I ask, my voice low and controlled.

He smirks, a gesture that irks me. "Just wanted to say hello to an old friend," he replies, his tone laced with mockery.

I don't have time for this. "If that's all, then I'm leaving," I say, turning to walk away.

Karl reaches out, grabbing my arm. "Not so fast, Ivan. Boris wants to talk to you." He holds out a phone, the screen showing a call in progress.

Boris. The name alone is enough to set my nerves on edge. Reluctantly I take the phone, holding it to my ear. "Boris," I greet, my tone icy.

"Ivan, my boy," Boris' voice oozes through the speaker, a mix of familiarity and threat. "I've heard about your little wedding and honeymoon. Quite the catch you've got yourself there. A real hot babe, I hear."

His words make my blood boil. The fact that he's been spying on me, on Julie, is a violation I can't tolerate. "What do you want, Boris?" I demand.

His chuckle is cold, devoid of humor. "I told you weeks ago that I have a job for you, Ivan. Something only you can handle. And you're going to do it, or else your lovely wife might find herself in a bit of trouble."

The threat is unmistakable. My grip tightens on the phone, anger coursing through me. "You leave her out of this," I growl.

"Oh, I will, as long as you cooperate," Boris replies, his voice a serpent's hiss.

I end the call without another word, my mind racing. There's no way I'm getting involved with the Bratva again, not after everything I've done to distance myself from that life. But Boris' threat to Julie changes everything.

I hand the phone back to Karl, my expression stone-cold. "Tell Boris he can go to hell," I say, and then I turn and walk away, leaving them sitting there.

As I rejoin Julie at the table, I can feel her eyes on me, filled with concern. "Is everything okay?" she asks, her voice tinged with worry.

I force a smile, one that doesn't quite reach my eyes. "Everything's fine," I lie, hoping to sound convincing. "Just some old business acquaintances."

But Julie isn't easily fooled. She studies me, her expression thoughtful, her eyes searching for the truth. "If you say so," she says, but there's a note of skepticism in her voice.

I nod, trying to push away the dark thoughts swirling in my mind. Boris' threat hangs over me like a dark cloud, but I'm determined to protect Julie, to keep her safe from the shadows of my past.

I'll do whatever it takes to ensure that the Bratva never gets near her. She's become more than just my wife in name; she's become a part of my life I'm not willing to lose.

CHAPTER 22

JULIE

Sitting on the cold, paper-covered table in the doctor's office, I can't help but let my mind wander. A month has passed since our honeymoon, and it feels like a lifetime and a blink of an eye all at once. My feet dangle off the edge of the table, and I play with the hem of the paper gown, a flimsy barrier that's as much a source of modesty as it is a reminder of why I'm here.

Ivan. The man who's been occupying my thoughts day and night. Evenings together in our transformed house have become a mix of cozy domesticity and frustrating distance. He's there, but not always present, buried in his work, his laptop an ever-present barrier.

And then there are the secrets, the shadows that seem to cling to him. The late-night phone calls that he brushes off, the strange men approaching him on the street. It happened again last week, and it left me with more questions than answers. Whenever I ask, he assures me it's nothing, but I can tell he's holding back.

But today, all of that takes a back seat to the reason I'm at the doctor's office. I'm pretty sure I'm pregnant. It's a strange feeling, a mix of excitement and apprehension. The thought of carrying Ivan's child, of starting this next new chapter, is both thrilling and terrifying. And to think, it might have happened on our first time on the plane. The memory brings a giggle to my lips, a sound that's half nerves, half amusement.

"Everything okay in here?" the doctor asks as she enters the room, pulling me from my reverie.

I clamp my hand over my mouth, suddenly feeling like a schoolgirl caught passing notes in class. "Yes, it's fine. Just, you know, doctor's office jitters," I reply, trying to sound nonchalant.

The doctor gives me a knowing smile as she pulls up my file on her tablet. "Well, let's see if we can alleviate some of those jitters. You mentioned you think you might be pregnant?"

I nod and nervously shift my weight, the paper gown crinkling with the movement. "Yeah, I'm pretty sure. My cycle's like clockwork, and it's been more than a little off since the honeymoon."

The doctor nods, her expression professional but kind. "Alright, we'll do a test and see what it says. How have you been feeling otherwise? Any morning sickness or other symptoms?"

I shrug, a little sheepish. "A bit of nausea here and there, and I've been craving pickles like crazy. I mean, I always liked them, but now it's like I *need* them."

She chuckles, making a few notes. "Cravings can be a tell-tale sign. We'll do a blood test as well, just to be sure."

As she prepares the test, I can't help but let my mind wander back to Ivan. What will he say when I tell him? Will he be excited, nervous, or just dive into planning mode like he does with everything else? And what about these secrets he's keeping? Will they change anything between us, especially now with a baby potentially on the way?

I take a deep breath, trying to calm the whirlwind of thoughts.

One step at a time, Julie. First, let's confirm this pregnancy, and then... well, then we'll figure out the rest.

Breaking into the bright light of day, I step out of the doctor's office, my heart pounding. I'm definitely pregnant. The news still rings in my ears, echoing with each step I take.

As I make my way to the parking lot, my mind races with thoughts of how to break the news to Ivan. I can't wait to see the look on his face. I almost skip to the car, a sleek, black Mercedes-Benz GLE that Ivan insisted I have.

"No wife of mine is riding the subway," he had declared with that typical mix of arrogance and concern. I have to admit, I've grown quite fond of its smooth ride and luxurious interior. Barb teases me about getting spoiled, but hey, who wouldn't love this kind of pampering?

I'm just about to open the door when a voice stops me dead in my tracks. "Mrs. Stepanov?" The accent is heavy, unmistakable. I turn, my heart skipping a beat as I see two men approaching.

I recognize them both from that day in Ivan's office when he proposed. Though I'd been ushered out before their meeting had taken place, I recall that Ivan had not been happy to see them.

The fact that they are approaching me now has my teeth set on edge.

"How was your appointment?" the one I remember Ivan addressing as Boris asks.

My heartbeat quickens, alarm surging through me. "I'm sorry, what did you just say?" I ask, my voice edged with disbelief. How could he possibly know about my doctor's appointment?

"It's a simple question," he presses, those beady eyes scrutinizing me closely. "How was your visit to the doctor?"

I take a step back, my mind racing. "That's none of your business," I retort, trying to mask the unease bubbling up inside me.

I make a move to open my car door but he's quick, stepping in front of me, effectively blocking my way. His size is intimidating, and his next words turn my blood to ice.

"We'll be escorting you back to your husband's office," he says, the tone of his voice leaving no room for argument.

For a brief moment I consider screaming, drawing attention, but his next warning stops me cold. "I wouldn't make a fuss if I were you. We wouldn't want you to have an unfortunate accident."

Between his tone and the look in his eyes, I believe him. Boris isn't bluffing, and the threat is real. My mind races, trying to find a way out, but I know I'm trapped. The other man, named Sergei, if memory serves, is silent but equally menacing. He slides into the driver's seat of my car, starting the engine with an ominous purr.

Boris ushers me into the backseat, his hand firm on my arm. The door closes with a finality that seals my fate. I'm in the car, Boris beside me, his presence a heavy weight that stifles any hope of escape.

The car ride is a tense, silent journey. Boris watches me closely, his gaze unrelenting. I sit as far away from him as the space allows, every nerve on edge, every sense heightened. I don't know what awaits me at Ivan's office, but I know one thing for sure—I have to warn him somehow.

The streets pass in a blur, each turn taking me further away from safety and deeper into uncertainty. My thoughts are with Ivan, our unborn child, and the life we've started to build.

A life that's now under threat by this man and whatever dark past he represents.

CHAPTER 23

IVAN

Jonathan Kline, the newest addition to my team, is proving to be an interesting character. He's sharp, a quick study that's impressive. There's a certain ambition in his eyes, a gleam that speaks of aspirations beyond being an assistant.

It's a trait I recognize and respect, reminding me of myself in my earlier days. I plan to keep a close watch on him; talent like his could be invaluable but being overly ambitious can lead to recklessness.

As I step into my office, I immediately notice Julie's absence. She had mentioned something about an extended lunch, but the specifics were lost in the rush of the day's activities. It's unusual for her to be away this long, and a part of me is curious about what she's up to.

Over the past weeks, since our return from Bora Bora, I've found myself increasingly attuned to her comings and goings, a development that would have surprised me at one point but now comes naturally.

My thoughts are interrupted by a soft knock on the door, and Jonathan steps in. "Mr. Stepanov, I've organized the files for the Winford project as you requested. Is there anything else you need?"

"Good work, Jonathan," I say, glancing over the neatly arranged files. "Keep an eye on that account; it's a key project for us. I want regular updates."

"Understood, sir," Jonathan replies, his eagerness evident. "I won't let you down."

As he leaves I lean back in my chair, my mind drifting back to Julie. Her extended lunch is out of character, and an inexplicable sense of unease begins to gnaw at me. I've become accustomed to her presence, her energy. I am unsettled when she is not around.

I decide to give her a call to check-in and make sure she's alright. The phone rings and I wait, expecting her cheerful voice to greet me. But it goes to voicemail, and I'm left with a lingering sense of disquiet.

Something doesn't feel right. It's a feeling I can't shake, a sense that something is amiss. I've learned to trust my instincts, they've kept me alive and successful in a world where a moment's hesitation can mean disaster.

I stand up, my decision made. I'm going to find my wife, to make sure she's not in trouble. The thought of her in any kind of distress is unacceptable, a risk I'm not willing to take.

The moment the office door swings open without a knock, I expect to see Julie, her usual spontaneous entrance accompanied by a bright smile. But what greets me instead causes the blood in my veins to turn to ice. Boris stands there, Julie with him, his hand gripping her arm with a possessiveness that sends a surge of fury through me. Sergei looms behind him, an ever-menacing presence.

Julie's expression is a mix of fear and defiance, a clear indication that she's been coerced into this situation. The sight of her in distress, at the mercy of these men, ignites a protective rage within me, a primal urge to shield her from harm.

Before I can react, Jonathan bursts into the room, his face etched with concern. "Mr. Stepanov, do you need me to call security?" he asks, his eyes darting between me and the unwelcome intruders.

Boris responds before I can. "There is no need for that, young man. We're just here for a friendly chat with Mr. Stepanov."

The casualness of his tone, the audacity to invade my space and threaten my wife, fuels my anger. I give Jonathan a nod, a silent signal to leave but stay alert. Jonathan hesitates for a split second, his gaze shifting from me to Julie, then back to the intruders. With a final wary look, he steps out of the room, but his departure is reluctant, a clear indication that he's ready to act if needed.

As soon as the door closes, the room becomes a charged arena, the tension stifling. Boris' smirk is infuriating, but it's Julie's well-being that's my primary concern. I take a step forward, my posture controlled yet imposing, my eyes fixed on Boris.

"Get your fucking hands off of my wife," I growl, my voice cold and steady despite the turmoil inside me.

Julie remains silent, her eyes meeting mine for a brief moment. There's a soundless plea in her gaze, one of fear but also trust. She knows I won't let anything happen to her, and that unspoken understanding solidifies my resolve.

Boris' eyes flicker with amusement, enjoying the control he believes he has. "We'll get to that, Ivan. But first, let's make sure we understand each other. Your lovely wife here," he tightens his grip on Julie's arm, "is a reminder of what's at stake."

Julie, with a sudden burst of defiance, wrenches her arm from Boris' grip and rushes to my side. Her proximity brings a measure of relief, yet the fear in her eyes, underlined by a burning anger, is a stark reminder of the danger we're in. A sick feeling overcomes me as I realize how vulnerable we are.

"Are you alright?" I ask, my voice laced with concern as I scan her for any signs of harm. She nods, her eyes turbulent, a storm of emotions swirling within them. The anger seems to outweigh her fear, and it's directed as much at me as it is at Boris.

"What the hell is going on, Ivan?" Julie demands, stepping back from me. The distance she puts between us stings more than I care to admit, a physical manifestation of the growing rift this situation has caused.

I don't have an immediate answer for her. My focus shifts back to Boris, the instigator of this chaos. "Who the fuck do you think you are?" I growl, the anger in my voice barely contained.

He seems unfazed by my hostility, his expression one of smug satisfaction. "Clearly, you didn't grasp the seriousness of the business proposition I offered you," he says, his tone casual but laced with menace. "However, I believe you now understand exactly how serious it is."

His words hang in the air, a blatant threat causing my spine to stiffen. This isn't just a simple power play; it's a calculated move to drag me back into a world I've fought hard to leave behind.

I keep my gaze locked on Boris, my mind racing for a solution. Julie's safety is paramount, and I need to navigate this situation carefully. Bori's presence here, his boldness in confronting me at my office, is a clear sign that he's not going to back down easily.

"I understood your offer, Boris," I say, maintaining a steady voice. "But I'll say it again, I'm not interested. I left that life behind. I've told you that multiple times already."

His smirk widens, a predator enjoying the hunt. "That's where you're wrong, Ivan. You don't get to decide whether or not you can leave that life. It's a part of you, and now," he glances at Julie, "it's a part of your wife's life too."

The implied threat to Julie nearly drives me to do something stupid. I step closer to her, wanting to shield her from whatever Boris has planned. Julie's presence here, used as a pawn in Boris' game, changes everything. I have to tread carefully, but I'm not going to let him use her to control me.

"You're playing a dangerous game, Boris," I warn, my voice low and full of venom.

He chuckles, clearly enjoying the upper hand. "I've always enjoyed a good game, Ivan. Especially when the stakes are high. And right now, they couldn't be higher."

Julie's confusion is tangible, her voice tinged with fear. "What proposition? And what life did you leave behind?" she asks, her words aimed at me but her eyes never leaving Boris.

Boris' response is swift and sharp, his voice cutting through the tension in the room. "Keeping secrets from your woman, Ivan?" he tsks.

"Julie, stay out of this," I say, my voice firmer than I intended. I see the hurt flash in her eyes, and I know I'm going to pay for those words later, but right now, her safety is my priority.

Without another word, Boris strides over to my desk and places an envelope on the surface. It appears thick and heavy with the weight of whatever instructions lie within. "Everything you need to know is in there," he says, his tone casual but his eyes cold. "The Bratva will compensate you well for this job."

The mention of the Bratva confirms my worst fear—that Boris is here to drag me back into a world I thought I had escaped. The Bratva is not an organization you simply walk away from, and their confirmed involvement complicates things further.

Julie remains silent, the shock of Boris' words still lingering. I can sense her unease, her fear, and it fuels my resolve to protect her from whatever he has planned.

My hand trembles with barely contained rage as I reach for the envelope, every muscle in my body coiled tight, ready to launch it back at Boris with all the contempt I feel. But Boris, perceptive and calculating, senses my intention and halts me with a chilling warning.

"Think carefully before you act, Ivan," he says, his voice laced with menace. His eyes shift to Julie, and the leer that he gives her makes my blood boil. "The Bratva knows what you value now," he adds, his words like a knife twisting in my gut.

The implication is clear and terrifying. They know about Julie, about her importance to me, and they're not above using her as leverage. It's a game of power and control, and Boris holds the cards.

His next words are a chilling reminder of the stakes. "Be wise, my friend. Consider the job because the alternative..." He lets the threat hang in the air, an unspoken but understood promise of violence and ugliness.

With that, Boris and Sergei turn and leave my office, their departure leaving heavy implications in their wake. The door closes with a soft click, but the echo of their threat reverberates through the room.

I stand there, envelope in hand, my blood boiling, mind racing. The danger is real and immediate, not just for me but for Julie as well. The Bratva's reach is long, their methods ruthless. I've spent years building a life away from their influence, but now they've managed to pull me back in, and Julie is caught in the crossfire.

CHAPTER 24

IVAN

"What the hell is going on, Ivan?" she demands, her voice sharp, cutting through the silence in the room. Her eyes, usually so warm, so understanding, now bore into me with an intensity that demands truth.

The tremors in Julie's body show the fear coursing through her, but it's her anger that resonates more profoundly. She's literally shaking, her eyes ablaze with a mixture of fear and fury. I reach out, trying to bridge the gap between us, to offer some semblance of comfort.

But she recoils, stepping away from me once more. Her withdrawal stings, more than I care to admit.

I know I can't keep evading her questions. But how do I explain a past so dark, so dangerous, without dragging her further into the mire? "It's complicated," I say, my voice steady but lacking conviction.

Her glare intensifies, and I can see the frustration building within her. "That's bullshit, Ivan. Stop lying to me. Am I in danger? Is Barb in danger?" Her voice cracks slightly, betraying the fear beneath her anger.

The question hangs heavily in the air, a stark reminder of the threat that now shadows our lives. "You won't be," I say, trying to sound more confident than I feel. "Neither will your aunt. I'll make sure of it."

But my answer only seems to fuel her frustration. "What the hell does that mean?" she snaps, her patience wearing thin.

I take a deep breath, knowing I owe her the truth, or at least as much of it as I can share without putting her in more danger. "Julie, it's complicated. My past with the Bratva... it's something I thought I'd left behind. They're not people you walk away from easily. And now, they've come back, and they're using you to get to me."

Julie looks at me, her eyes searching for assurance in my words. I can see the conflict within her, the struggle to reconcile the man she knows with the shadows of the man I used to be.

"So you're a Russian mobster?" she asks. I note the lack of surprise in her tone.

"I was. A long time ago. But I left that world."

She chuckles but it holds no humor. "Boris seems to disagree with you on that."

"I'll handle this, Julie," I say, my voice firm. "Trust me. I'll find a way to protect us both from whatever he has planned."

The tension in the air grows thick as I try to navigate the conversation, my mind desperately searching for solutions.

"I'm sending you to my cabin upstate. It's remote and safe. You'll be out of harm's way until I handle this."

Her response is immediate and fierce. "You're not sending me anywhere, Ivan. I'm not some package to be shipped off for safekeeping." Her stance is defiant, her eyes ablaze with a determination both admirable and frustrating.

I try to reason with her, to explain the gravity of the situation. "Julie, you don't understand the kind of danger we're dealing with. The Bratva isn't just some street gang; they're a powerful criminal organization with a very long reach."

Her face falls, a look of betrayal and hurt that cuts deeper than any physical wound could. "Ivan, why didn't you tell me this before? How could you keep something like this from me?"

I reach out to her, but again she steps back, her trust in me clearly shaken. "I thought I could protect you from it, keep it buried. I didn't want my past to taint the life we're trying to build together."

"But now it has," she whispers, her voice barely audible. "And you think sending me away will fix this?"

I shake my head, struggling to find the words to convey the depth of my concern for her safety. "It's not about fixing it, Julie. It's about keeping you safe. I can't risk anything happening to you."

Her eyes glisten with unshed tears, a turmoil of emotions playing across her face. "And what about you, Ivan? Who's going to keep you safe?"

I set my jaw, a resolve firming within me. "I'll handle Boris and the Bratva. I'll find a way to end this, once and for all.

But I need to know you're out of the danger zone first. Please, Julie, trust me on this."

Julie's stance is resolute, her eyes demanding honesty. "If you want me to trust you, I need to know everything. All of it. I need to know who you really are."

I take a deep breath, knowing that the time for keeping secrets has passed. "It all started with my father's death," I begin, my voice heavy as memories I've long tried to bury begin to resurface. "He was killed by a powerful Bratva in Russia. My mother, my brother, Fyodor and I had to flee. We ended up here, in New York. It was a hard life and we struggled to make ends meet."

Her expression softens slightly, but her gaze remains intense, urging me to continue.

"I was young, angry, and desperate," I confess. "That's when I got involved with the Mikhailov Bratva. They offered protection, a sense of belonging, and a way to make money. It was easy to get into as it was what I knew from my homeland. I was good at it, too good. I climbed the ranks, did things I'm not proud of."

Julie swallows hard, her eyes reflecting the shock of my revelations. "But how did you get from there to here? To being a respected businessman?"

"That came later," I explain, meeting her gaze. "The former leader of the Bratva, he saw potential in me beyond the criminal world. He released me from my obligations after I'd made them millions and secured enough for myself to start anew. That's when I started my company. I left that world behind, Julie. I haven't been involved in any criminal activities for over a decade."

Her brow furrows, a mix of understanding and disbelief. "If you were relieved of your obligation, why does Boris think you're still beholden to them? Why come after you now?"

I shake my head, frustration evident in my tone. "I don't know. Maybe there's been a power shift within the Bratva, or maybe they just never truly let anyone go. But one thing's clear, they're using my past to manipulate me now."

Julie steps closer, her anger subsiding into concern. "Ivan, this is serious. You can't just handle this on your own. We need to go to the police, get protection."

I hesitate, the thought of involving law enforcement a complicated one. "It's not that simple. Going to the police could escalate things. I need to handle this carefully, strategically."

"But what about us? What about our safety?" Her voice trembles slightly, betraying her fear yet again.

I reach out, taking her hands in mine. "I'll do everything in my power to protect you. I won't let anything happen to you, Julie. That's a promise."

I squeeze her hands gently, trying to convey my determination. "I'll find a way to end this threat, once and for all. I have resources, connections. I'm not that young, desperate boy anymore. I'm a man with something to fight for now—you, our family, this business. I won't let the Bratva destroy what I've built, what we've built together."

Julie nods, a silent understanding passing between us. "Just... just be careful, Ivan. I don't want to lose you."

I pull her into a hug, holding her close. "You won't lose me. We're in this together. We'll get through this, I promise."

Settling onto the sofa, I hold Julie's hand gently, grateful that she hasn't pulled away. Her presence, her touch, it's a calming lifeline in the chaos that's threatening to engulf us.

Her hand tightens around mine, her resolve clear. "Then I'm staying with you. Like you said, we're in this together. We'll face this together."

The thought of placing her in the direct path of danger is unbearable. "No, Julie. It's too risky. I couldn't bear it if something happened to you because of me."

She searches my face, her own determination matching mine. "And I can't bear the thought of being safe while you're here, facing this alone. We're in this together, Ivan. For better or worse."

Her words strike a chord deep within me. She's right—we're a team, in every sense of the word. But the thought of her in harm's way is agonizing.

I take a deep breath, weighing my options. "Alright. We'll go to the cabin together. It'll give us some time away from the city, away from prying eyes. We can plan our next move from there."

She nods, a small smile of relief crossing her lips. "Thank you, Ivan. That means everything to me."

"But first," I continue, "I need to talk to Fyodor. He's not just my brother; he's my closest ally. If anyone can help us navigate this situation, it's him."

Julie leans into me, her presence a comforting warmth. "Then let's do it. Let's talk to Fyodor and figure out our strategy."

I wrap my arm around her, drawing her close. In her embrace, I find strength. Together, we'll face whatever comes our way.

CHAPTER 25

JULIE

I'm still reeling from the revelation that my husband—the man I'm undeniably falling for—has a past tangled up with the Russian mafia. On top of that, the news of my pregnancy has my head spinning.

With all that's going on, all the danger that surrounds us, I'm wondering if now is the right time to tell Ivan that I'm pregnant.

Sliding into the passenger seat of the company car, a sleek and shiny BMW, I can't help but feel a twinge of unease. The driver, a suited, tough-looking man with sunglasses, gives me a brief nod before starting the car. He's the silent, stoic type, probably one of Ivan's security guys, his presence both reassuring and intimidating.

I take a deep breath, trying to calm the thoughts swirling in my head. I need to pack for our unexpected retreat to the cabin, but first, there's a necessary detour I need to make. Despite Ivan's concerns for safety, I have to see Barb. I need the kind of strength and wisdom that only she can provide.

When we pull up outside Barb's place, the driver parks the car and exits with quick efficiency. Before I know it, he's standing at my door offering me a steadying hand.

I nod, appreciating his vigilance. "Thank you," I reply, stepping out of the car. His presence is a stark reminder of the new reality I'm facing in a world where I'm whisked around by silent bodyguards and my movements are monitored for safety.

Barb's place is as welcoming as ever, her latest array of paintings adding splashes of color and life to the cozy apartment. She's surprised to see me, her artist's eyes quickly picking up on my unsettled state and the dark, silent man accompanying me.

"Julie, what's wrong, honey?" she asks, her voice laced with concern.

I spill everything without hesitation—the pregnancy, Ivan's past, the encounter with Boris. It all comes tumbling out in a rush. Barb listens intently, her expression shifting from shock to concern to that steely determination that I've always admired.

"First things first," she says, standing up. "You and that baby are the priority. If Ivan thinks this cabin is the safest place for you, then you should go. But" her eyes harden, "you make sure that man does everything in his power to keep you safe. And if he needs a piece of my mind to inspire him, he'll get it.

"Secondly, congratulations! I'm so excited to be a great auntie!" I nod, a grin breaking across my face despite the chaos of the day.

"Thanks. Can you believe it?"

Barb rushes over, enveloping me in a hug that's both protective and bursting with happiness. "This is wonderful news!" she exclaims, pulling back to look at me, her eyes shimmering with unshed tears. "A little miracle!"

I laugh, the sound mingling with wonderment and a touch of disbelief. "It's pretty crazy, isn't it? A month ago I was single with no prospects and now..."

Barb holds my hands, her own trembling slightly with excitement. "Julie, this is a blessing. I know things are complicated right now, but this baby is a sign of hope, of new beginnings."

We sit down together, the joy of the moment enveloping us amidst the uncertainty of the situation. "I can't wait to spoil him or her rotten," she says.

I squeeze her hands, my heart swelling with love and gratitude. "They're going to love their great-aunt Barb," I say, my voice catching. "And they're going to hear all about how you've been there for us, through thick and thin."

For a moment, we forget the looming threat of Boris, lost in the joy of the new life that is on the way. It's a brief respite, a cherished oasis of happiness in a desert of worry and uncertainty.

The doorbell's chime is abrupt, slicing through the quiet of Barb's home. My newfound security detail moves with a silent efficiency that's both reassuring and slightly unnerving. I watch as he answers the door, his posture alert, every inch the trained protector Ivan has assigned to me.

As the door swings open, a disheveled figure steps into view. He's grungy, with unkempt hair and a weary look that speaks of hard living. His clothes are worn, and there's a desperation in his eyes that's alarming. Something about him strikes a chord of recognition, but I can't quite place him.

Before I can ponder further, Barb's sharp voice cuts through the air like a knife. "Calvin?" she hisses, her tone a mix of disbelief and rising anger. "What the hell are you doing here?"

Calvin. The name jolts me, sending a shockwave through my body. Calvin, my father, the man responsible for my mother's death. It's been two decades since I've seen the man and yet here he is, standing in my aunt's living room.

My guard steps forward, his body language ready to intervene, but my father's plea stops everyone in their tracks. "Please, Barb," he begs, his voice hoarse with emotion. "I just want to see my daughter. She's all I have left."

I stare at him, a tumult of emotions crashing over me. Anger, confusion, a curious sense of detachment.

The guard positions himself between my father and me. He glances over his shoulder in my direction as if wordlessly sending the message that he'll fold my father in half and toss him in the trash the second I ask. It's an offer that's hard to resist.

Barb narrows her eyes. "How the hell did you even know she was here?"

My father appears sheepish. "I've been keeping an eye on this place," he says before turning to me. "I know you and your aunt have always been close, Julie. I figured that if I stayed nearby, it'd be only a matter of time before I saw my little girl again."

Barb's face is a mask of fury, her hands clenched at her sides. "You lost the right to call her your little girl the day you killed her mother," she spits out, her voice trembling with barely contained rage.

"It was an accident!" he raises his voice.

"Bullshit," Barb responds in a like tone.

My father looks defeated, his shoulders slumping as he absorbs Barb's words. His eyes, hollow and haunted, shift to me, seeking some semblance of recognition, of connection. But all I feel is a hollow emptiness, a void where paternal love should have been.

The air in the room feels charged, heavy with the burden of years of unspoken pain. My father stands there, a figure of remorse and desperation, his eyes pleading for something that feels impossible to give.

"I know you have every right to hate me, Julie," he says, his voice quivering with emotion. "And I wouldn't blame you if you did. But I'm not the man I used to be. I've found God, turned my life around. All I'm asking for is a chance to tell you how sorry I am. To make amends for the unforgivable."

His words hang in the air, a desperate plea from a man seeking redemption. But the scars he left, the wounds he inflicted, they run deep, deeper than mere apologies can heal.

Barb's skepticism is palpable, her stance firm and protective. "Sorry doesn't change the past, Calvin. It doesn't bring her back," she says, her voice steady but laced with a bitterness born from years of carrying the weight of loss and betrayal.

I stand torn between the man claiming to be my father and the lifetime of hurt he's responsible for. He's a stranger to me, yet his presence stirs a turmoil of emotions I can't quite comprehend.

"I've lived without parents basically my whole life, without the family I should have had. And it's all because of you," I say, my voice barely above a whisper, yet carrying the weight of decades of pain. "How can you just expect me to accept your apology? To believe that you've changed?"

My father's face crumples, the lines etched with a lifetime of regret and sorrow. "I can't change the past, Julie. I know that. I live with that guilt every day. But I'm here now, asking for forgiveness, asking for a chance to at least try to make things right."

The tension in the room escalates as Calvin's demeanor shifts, his desperation giving way to a more aggressive stance. It's a startling transformation that reveals the complexity of the man standing before us.

"Julie, please," he implores, his voice edging on insistence. "I'm not asking for much. Just a chance to talk, to explain myself."

I shake my head, my resolve firm. "I can't, not now. This is all too much. I need time."

He takes a step closer, his frustration evident. "I've waited years for this moment, Julie. Don't shut me out now. I'm your father, for God's sake!"

His claim, meant to bridge the gap between us, only serves to widen it further. The guard, a silent sentinel until now, steps forward, his presence a silent warning. Calvin's eyes flicker to him, and for a moment a flash of the man he claims he no longer is surfaces, a glimpse of the anger and violence that once defined him.

But he checks himself, the anger dissipating as quickly as it appeared. He reaches into his pocket, pulling out a piece of paper with a number scrawled on it. He extends it toward me, his hand trembling slightly.

"Here. This is my number. Call me when you're ready to talk. Please, Julie. I'm begging you."

His voice is a mix of desperation and hope, a plea from a man seeking redemption from the daughter he never really knew. I don't respond, my silence speaking volumes. He stares at me for a moment longer, searching for a sign, any indication of forgiveness. But I offer none.

With a heavy sigh he turns and walks away, his shoulders slumped in defeat. The door closes behind him, leaving us in the aftermath of an unexpected encounter that has created an uproar in mere minutes.

"Julie," Barb says, turning to me. "I'm so, so sorry for that. I had no idea he was going to just barge in here."

I'm stunned. I don't know what to say, don't know how to even begin processing what just happened, my father reappearing out of the blue.

"Did you know he was out?" That's all I can think to say.

After he killed my mother, my father was arrested and ultimately convicted of involuntary manslaughter. He was sentenced to twenty years in prison.

My aunt's expression softens as she meets my gaze. "Yes, I knew he'd been released," she admits, her voice tinged with regret. "But I honestly hoped he'd be smart enough to stay away. I thought he'd understand that you wanted nothing to do with him."

Her eyes drop, and I can see the weight of her decision of not telling me pressing down on her. "I should've told you, sweetheart. I should have prepared you for the possibility of him showing up. I just... I wanted to protect you from more pain. I'm so sorry."

I can see the sincerity in her eyes, the genuine remorse. Barb has always been my protector, the one constant in a life marked by loss and uncertainty. I know her intentions were to shield me, even if it meant keeping me in the dark about Calvin's release.

"It's okay," I say, reaching out to grasp her hands. "You've always looked out for me. I know you didn't mean any harm. And honestly, I'm not even sure what I would've done with that information."

Barb looks up, her eyes meeting mine. "I just didn't want his shadow to darken your life again, Julie. After everything you've been through, you deserve peace."

I squeeze her hands, grateful for her unwavering support and love. "I have peace, thanks to you and Ivan. Calvin can't take that away from me. Not anymore." Another thought occurs to me, an unsettling one. "Are you okay? Are you safe here with him knowing where you live?"

Barb's response is immediate, her voice laced with the fearless strength I've always admired. "That man doesn't scare me, Julie. He wouldn't dare fuck with me, not now, not ever. His best days are long behind him."

Her confidence is infectious, a balm to my chaotic state of nerves. Yet despite her bravado, a part of me wishes for that same fearlessness. The encounter with my father has left me shaken.

"I wish I had your courage, Barb," I admit, a small smile tugging at the corner of my lips.

Barb steps closer, her hands gripping my shoulders firmly. "You have more strength than you realize, Julie. You're facing all of this head-on, and that takes guts. You're a fighter, just like me, just like your mom."

Her words are a comfort, a reminder of the resilience that runs in our family. I nod, drawing strength from her unwavering support.

"I should get going," I say, the reality of my own situation pressing in. "Ivan's waiting for me, and we have a lot to figure out."

Barb pulls me into a tight embrace, her arms wrapping around me in a protective cocoon. "You go and sort things out with that husband of yours. And remember, I'm always here for you, no matter what. Please stay safe."

I hug her back, grateful for her presence in my life. "Thanks, Aunt Barb. I don't know what I'd do without you."

Breaking away from the embrace, I head toward the door, my mind a tempest of thoughts. The encounter with Calvin, the looming threat of Boris, the pregnancy, it's a lot to process. But I know I'm not alone. I have Barb, Ivan, and the strength that's always been a part of me, even when I've doubted it.

I step out of Barb's apartment, the guard by my side, and I take a deep breath. It's time to face whatever comes next, to protect my growing family and confront the shadows of the past.

CHAPTER 26

JULIE

The ride over to Ivan's office is a blur. I can't help but feel a sense of safety with my driver despite my irritation that Ivan hadn't mentioned his true role.

"Hey," I say, leaning forward to catch the driver's eye in the rearview mirror. "I need you to do something for me."

He meets my gaze, a silent question in his eyes.

"Please don't tell Ivan about my father showing up at Barb's," I plead, my voice firm. "He has enough on his plate, and I don't want to add to it."

The driver hesitates, his expression unreadable behind the sunglasses. I can tell he's weighing his loyalty to Ivan against my request.

After a moment he gives a slight nod. "I won't mention it, Mrs. Stepanov," he says, his voice a low rumble. "But if Mr. Stepanov asks directly if something happened, I can't lie to him."

I slump back in my seat, a mix of relief and trepidation washing over me. "Thank you," I whisper, more to myself than to him.

The sleek car pulls up to Ivan's office in the bustling Financial District, and my heart begins to beat a little faster. As if the driver can sense my nervousness, he looks over his shoulder and says, "We're here, Mrs. Stepanov," in a voice that's as calm and collected as his demeanor.

After parking the car, the driver opens my door and offers his hand, immediately at my side like a protective shadow. Upon exiting the vehicle, I see Ivan emerge from the building. He's a striking figure against the backdrop of the city, tall and confident in his tailored suit that fits him like a glove. The look on his face when he sees me sends warmth spreading through me—relief, concern, affection—they're all there, written in the lines of his face and in the intensity of his gaze.

The concern in Ivan's eyes grows as he reaches me, his hands gently framing my face. "Is everything okay?" His voice is laced with a protective edge, his gaze searching mine for any hint of distress.

I shake my head in the affirmative, forcing a small smile to reassure him. "I'm fine, Ivan, really. Just a bit shaken from everything."

His eyes continue to probe, looking for the truth in mine. Finding no trace of deceit, he pulls me close, wrapping his arms around me in a tight, protective embrace. I sink into his hold, allowing myself to feel the safety and comfort he offers.

As he holds me, a part of me debates whether or not to tell him about the encounter with Calvin. But another part, the part that feels safe and cherished in his arms, decides against it. Ivan would go to the ends of the earth to protect me, and I know he'd tear Calvin apart if I gave him any reason. I don't want to add to his burden.

So I keep the encounter to myself, choosing instead to bask in the sense of security that Ivan's presence brings. I find a haven in his arms, a place where the shadows of my past and the threats of the present can't reach me.

He nods, his gaze lingering on me with a mixture of emotions. "We need to get you to safety," he says, his tone firm. "The cottage is ready, I had my staff go ahead and prepare everything. We'll be safe there."

The journey is a quiet one, the tension of the day hanging heavy in the car. Ivan sits beside me, his presence both a comfort and constant reminder of the danger we're in. Every so often, he glances my way, his deep eyes filled with concern.

"Are you sure you're okay?" he asks for what must be the third time. His voice is gentle, but I can hear the underlying worry.

I nod, managing a small smile. "I'm alright. Just a lot to process, you know?" I reply, trying to sound more confident than I feel.

He reaches over, taking my hand in his. His touch is warm and reassuring, and as he lifts my hand to his lips, kissing my fingers softly, a wave of heat washes over me, momentarily pushing aside the fear and anxiety. It's amazing how his touch can make me forget the world and its troubles, if only for a moment.

We ride in silence for a while, the city gradually giving way to the scenic beauty of upstate New York. I find myself lost in thought, attempting to make sense of everything. I need to tell Ivan about the baby, but the timing never seems right.

Finally, the car turns down a narrow road, and we're surrounded by dense trees. The cabin appears, nestled in the woods, its simplicity belying the elegance within. It's a charming two-story structure, with a stone facade and large windows that offer a view of the surrounding forest. The wraparound porch is inviting, lined with comfortable chairs and a swing, perfect for enjoying the tranquility of nature.

Inside, the cabin is warm and welcoming. The living room boasts a large stone fireplace, plush sofas, and a soft rug underfoot. The decor is rustic yet modern, with touches of luxury that speak of Ivan's taste. Large windows let in natural light, offering stunning views of the woods outside. Kiki is already there, wasting no time coming up to me and curling around my leg in the way she always does when I come home.

"It's beautiful, Ivan," I say, my voice filled with genuine admiration as I take in the cozy interior.

He smiles, a look of relief crossing his face. "I'm glad you like it. I wanted somewhere safe and comfortable for us."

As we settle in, Ivan reveals that his brother, Fyodor, will be joining us the next day. I'm not sure how I feel about that. On one hand, it's more security, but on the other, it's a reminder of the danger we're in.

I look up at Ivan, his face etched with the weight of responsibility. In this moment, away from the chaos of the city, I see him not just as my husband or the CEO of a major company, but as a man caught in a situation he never wanted.

"I need to tell you something, Ivan," I begin, my heart pounding in my chest.

He looks at me, his expression softening. "What is it, Julie? You can tell me anything."

I take a deep breath, ready to reveal the truth about the baby and my encounter with my father. But before I can speak, the warmth of his hand on mine, the safety of the cabin, and the overwhelming events of the day catch up to me. And in that moment, all I want is him. The rest can wait.

"I need you, Ivan," I say, my voice low and filled with desire. "I need to feel alive, to feel loved."

His response is immediate, his arms wrapping around me, pulling me close. The heat between us reignites, pushing aside all of the fear and uncertainty.

He sets me down onto the big couch, the cushion soft beneath me. Ivan doesn't say a word, instead focusing on my eyes as he works the button and zipper of my pants. Once they're open, he slides them down my thighs along with my panties. The air is cool against my skin, and I watch as he begins by kissing my legs, moving closer to my inner thighs.

He knows just how to tease me, how to give me just what I want before I even know I want it.

With a smooth movement, he spreads my legs, his gaze drifting down to my womanhood.

"Is there any part of you that's not impossibly beautiful?" he asks.

I laugh. "Charm will get you everywhere."

"Good to know," he replies. "But I'm already in the exact place I want to be."

Without another word, he moves in and begins kissing me closer and closer to my pussy. He teases me with flicks of his tongue along my folds, as if he wants to make sure there's not a single part of me that goes unattended.

When he finally spreads me open and touches my most sensitive place, I'm on the verge of melting.

"There," I moan. "Just like that."

He doesn't need any guidance from me though, he knows just where to kiss, just where to lick, just where to suck. His fingers move inside me, my wetness guiding him deeper, his thumb making perfect circles on my clit. The orgasm builds and builds, and I crave release like nothing else.

I moan, squirming at his licks, touches, and kisses. Ivan raises his head, still fingering me as he speaks.

"Come for me. Right now."

He's impossible to resist. He goes back down, focusing his attention on my clit and that's all it takes. I release, my back arching as I allow inhibited shouts of total pleasure fill the cabin. He eats me out through the orgasm, licking up every last bit before standing up and wiping his mouth with the back of his hand.

"Turn over," he says. He's hard as hell, and it's clear what he wants.

"No," I pant. "You sit."

He grins. Normally, he's the one in control.

But now, I'm ready to be the one in the driver's seat.

CHAPTER 27

IVAN

Julie's a thing of beauty as she climbs on top of me. I watch the toned muscles of her legs work as she straddles me, her hand reaching down to grasp my cock as she gets into position.

"Someone's feeling bossy." I move my hands along her irresistible curves as she places my head at her slick opening.

She grins. "Careful— you sass me too much, and I tie you up."

That gets a laugh out of me. I'm more than pleased to see how well she's taken to our domination and submission play. Julie likes giving up control, but there's no mistaking her independence and will, even when she's tied up in front of me.

She moves my cock back and forth, closing her eyes and savoring the sensation of my hardness against her clit. I groan, the feeling pretty damn nice on my end, too. I put my hands on her hips, prepared to guide her down lower.

"Not so fast," she says. "I'm the one in control, remember?"

"How could I forget?"

Instead of guiding her down, I move my hands along her long, supple legs. Julie's body is perfect, utterly flawless. Every time with her is as exciting as the first. There's a true sexual connection between us, one I'd always been vaguely aware of long before I ever touched her.

I watch her rub herself with my head, her lips spreading as she drags me along her seam. She's moaning, her chest rising and falling. I can feel her heat, her wetness. She starts to shake, her full, round breasts, those perfect tits with their rosy-pink nipples, quivering before me. I can't resist leaning forward and taking one of them into my mouth, the delicious saltiness of her skin washing over my palate.

Is there any part of this woman that doesn't taste like heaven?

"Oh… Oh, Ivan…"

With that, her back makes one final, hard arch. She comes, her body shaking, her grip barely able to keep my cock in her hand. When she's done, she falls forward, her hair draping over both sides of her face, her breasts hanging heavy. She takes one deep breath, then another.

"Was that good for you?" I ask, my tone wry.

"Most definitely."

"Good. Now, if I'm not inside you in the next few seconds, I might lose my mind."

I put my hand on the small of her back, guiding her down my length. My cock finally pushes inside, the first few inches of her pussy gripping me tightly. I groan as she sinks down further until every bit of me is buried inside.

"God, you feel so damn good," I say as I clamp my hands onto her rear, unable to resist a squeeze of that perfect ass of hers.

She smiles in reply, her hips moving back and forth, the muscles of her core working in a most sensual way. I take hold of her tits, squeezing them firmly, teasing her nipples with my thumbs.

"Just like that," she moans as she rides me. "Just like that."

Her pace quickens, her breasts bouncing up and down.

"Come inside me, Ivan. "Please. I'm so close."

There's no sense in resisting. I feel myself reach the edge, holding there long enough so her own orgasm can take hold. She arches her back again and I allow myself to move over the line, pleasure ripping through me as I come. My cock pulses, my seed shooting deep inside of her. She keeps riding me through it all, coaxing out every last drop.

In the quiet aftermath of our passion, Julie rests beside me on the couch, her body a gentle curve against my side. The warmth of her presence, the soft rhythm of her breathing, it's a comfort that I've come to crave more than I ever thought possible. We lie in silence, the kind that speaks volumes, filled with a shared understanding and a connection that's grown deeper with every passing moment.

Those three little words linger on the tip of my tongue, echoing in the back of my mind. But I resist speaking them aloud, not yet ready to give them a voice. There's a part of me that's still guarded, still wary of the vulnerability that comes with such an admission. It's a battle between the instinct to protect myself and the growing realization of just how much Julie means to me.

She falls asleep, her breathing steady and peaceful. In the dim light of the cabin, her face is a picture of tranquility, a stark contrast to the storm of emotions and fears I know are swirling within her. The danger that looms over us, the shadow of my past life, it's a threat I never wanted her to face. But now that it's here, I vow to protect her, to shield her from the darkness that's encroaching on our lives.

I rise quietly, careful not to disturb her. Dressing in silence, I pause to kiss her forehead, a tender gesture that belies the turmoil inside me. She stirs slightly, a soft murmur escaping her lips, and for a moment, I'm tempted to stay, to keep watch over her as she sleeps. But there's work to be done, plans to be made. I scoop her off the couch and carry her upstairs to the bedroom. I know she needs rest, recovery. Kiki is close behind, curling around my legs as I move. When I set Julie down, the cat wastes no time hopping to her side.

Downstairs, the cabin is still, the only sound the occasional crackle of the dying fire. I take a seat by the window, my gaze scanning the darkness outside. The isolation is both a blessing and a curse—a sanctuary from the world, but also a place that feels increasingly like a fortress under siege.

My laptop sits open in front of me, a portal to the resources and connections I need to formulate a plan. My mind works methodically, piecing together strategies, contingencies, anything and everything I can do to neutralize the threat. Boris and his ilk, they're a cancer, a remnant of a life I left behind. But they've returned to claim a debt I never owed, targeting the one person who's become my reason for everything.

The night deepens as I work, the hours slipping away in a blend of determination and focus. I can't allow fear or doubt to cloud my judgment, not when so much is at stake. Julie, our future, the family we're going to build, they're the anchors that will keep me grounded, the reasons I'll fight with everything I have.

I glance at the clock, noting the passage of time, the approach of dawn. The world outside is still shrouded in darkness, but I know the light will come soon, bringing with it new challenges and new battles. But for now, I find strength in the knowledge that Julie is safe, asleep upstairs, her trust in me is a responsibility I don't take lightly.

CHAPTER 28

JULIE

I wake up to the familiar warmth of Kiki curled up beside me, her gentle purring a soothing contrast to the tornado swirling in my mind as soon as my eyes open. I stretch, feeling the pleasant soreness in my muscles, a physical reminder of last night's passion. Glancing around, I notice the other side of the bed is empty, the sheets cool to the touch. Ivan's not there.

Curiosity piques as I get up and move to the window of our cozy second-floor room. Peering out, I see that our car is missing, replaced by a different one, sleek and unfamiliar. A frown creases my forehead. Where did he go without telling me?

Shaking off the unease, I quickly dress, opting for comfort in a pair of jeans and a soft sweater. After a quick brush of my teeth and a hasty ponytail to tame my unruly hair, I'm ready to face the day, or at least try to.

Heading downstairs, the cabin feels larger, emptier without Ivan's presence. It's a beautiful place, rustic yet elegant, with large windows that flood the space with late morning light. But right now it feels more like a gilded cage, a luxurious confinement amidst the looming threat outside.

I tiptoe into the kitchen, my eyes fixed on a man rummaging through the fridge. He's got the same build as Ivan, so it's easy to assume it's him. Feeling playful, I sneak up behind him, a mischievous grin on my face. In one swift move, I reach out and goose him, erupting into giggles.

But as the man whirls around, my laughter dies in my throat. It's not Ivan. Instead, I'm met with the surprised face of Fyodor. I let out an embarrassed squeak, stepping back as my cheeks flush a deep shade of red.

"Oh my God, I'm sorry! I thought you were—" I stammer, but my apology is cut off as Ivan strides into the kitchen.

"What's going on here?" Ivan asks, his eyebrow raised in amusement.

Fyodor, still chuckling, looks between me and Ivan. "Well, your wife here just gave me quite the welcome."

I can feel my face burning with embarrassment. "I'm so sorry, Fyodor. I really thought you were Ivan," I say, wishing the floor would swallow me whole.

Fyodor winks at me, clearly not offended. "Don't worry about it. It's the most action I've had in weeks."

I let out a relieved laugh, feeling a bit more at ease. "I'll make sure to double-check next time before I decide to get frisky," I joke, trying to lighten the mood.

Ivan wraps an arm around my waist, pulling me close. "I think I'll have to keep a closer eye on you, Mrs. Stepanov. Can't have you assaulting my family members."

I lean into Ivan, still feeling a bit flustered but grateful for his good-natured teasing.

Fyodor stands there, his resemblance to Ivan striking yet distinct. He's leaner, his features less rugged, but there's no denying the family connection. His eyes have the same intensity, but there's a lightness to him that Ivan sometimes lacks.

"Why are you here, Fyodor?" I ask, curiosity getting the better of me.

Ivan answers, his tone serious. "He's here for extra protection, Julie."

We sit down at the kitchen table, a sense of urgency hanging in the air. Ivan and Fyodor start discussing the situation with Boris and the Bratva, brainstorming ideas and strategies. I listen, trying to keep up, but the weight of the conversation presses down on me. The reality of what we're up against, the danger lurking just beyond our peaceful getaway, is overwhelming.

As they talk, my mind drifts to our baby. This unborn child is the reason I have to be strong, to face this head-on. But the thought of bringing him or her into a world where threats like Boris exist makes my heart clench with fear.

"Ivan," I interrupt, my voice laced with concern. "What if this doesn't work? What if Boris doesn't back down?"

Ivan's expression softens as he turns to me. "Julie, I won't let anything happen to you. Whatever it takes, I'll protect you."

Fyodor adds, "And I'm here too. You're not in this alone."

"For now, however," Ivan says, "I would like to keep the details between my brother and me."

"What?" The word shoots out of my mouth. "As in, without me in the loop?"

Ivan takes a breath, closing his eyes. I can sense he's choosing his next words very carefully.

"You're not going to be out of the loop," he says.

"Sure as hell feels like that from where I'm sitting." I cross my arms, feeling a mix of frustration and worry. "I want to help, Ivan," I argue, trying to mask the anxiety creeping into my voice. I hate feeling sidelined, especially in a situation that's spiraling so dangerously close to us.

Ivan approaches me, his hand gently cradling my face. His touch is always reassuring, but right now, it feels like a barrier keeping me from the action. "Julie, I know you do, but this is something Fyodor and I need to handle," he says, his eyes searching mine for understanding. "We have unique skills, for lack of a better way of putting it."

Fyodor chimes in, "He's right, Julie. Dealing with the Bratva, it's a different ballgame altogether."

I can't help but feel a little dismissed, even though I know they're just trying to protect me. "I'm not just some damsel in distress, Ivan. I can handle myself," I say, a bit more sharply than I intend.

Ivan's gaze doesn't waver. He's always so damn composed. "I know you can. And that's not what this is about. It's about keeping you safe," he adds, his voice softening. "You'll be informed of every step, every decision. I promise," he reassures me.

Fyodor adds, "Besides, you have your own important work to do, right? Starting your non-profit. Ivan told me all about it."

I let out a sigh, feeling the fight drain out of me. They're right, but it doesn't make it any easier to swallow. "Alright, I'll focus on my project. But Ivan," I say, locking eyes with him, "you better keep your promise. No secrets, okay?"

His answer is a gentle kiss on my forehead, a gesture that always manages to soothe me. "No secrets," he says softly.

I head upstairs to get started on the non-profit. Once in the cozy room I've decided will be my office, I settle at the small desk by the window, my laptop open in front of me. The view outside is serene and calming. Starting a non-profit isn't easy. There's the business plan to refine, permits to obtain, paperwork to file, and a million other details. I take a deep breath, trying to channel my energy into something positive, something that can make a difference.

I'm about to dive into my work when I notice a missed call and message from Barb. She says that Calvin wants to meet, to talk and maybe have lunch. A wave of emotions flood through me—anger, curiosity, annoyance, as well as a strange sense of longing for a connection I've never had. I stare at the screen, unsure of how to respond.

For a long moment I just sit there, lost in thought. This is the man responsible for so much pain in my life, yet he's also a part of me in a way I can't deny. I tell her to give him my number along with a stern warning not to overuse it, and that I need time to process everything, to make a decision of whether or not I want to see him. This is something I need to discuss with Ivan first, to get his take on it. With everything else going on, the last thing I need is to navigate the complexities of a relationship with an absent father I've hated for most of my life.

I push the phone aside and turn my attention back to my laptop. The business plan for my non-profit stares back at me, a reminder of the future I'm trying to build. It's a future that's suddenly filled with more unknowns than ever—a husband with a dangerous past, a father seeking redemption, and a little life growing inside me.

As I delve into my work, the plans and projections, the mission statement and goals, I find a sense of purpose. This is more than just a project; it's a part of who I am, a way to make a difference in a world that seems increasingly chaotic. It's a chance to create something good, something lasting, amidst the uncertainty of our current situation.

Hours pass, the afternoon light shifting across the room as I work. The cabin is quiet, the only sounds the occasional murmur of voices from downstairs and the soft tapping of my keyboard. I'm deep in concentration, mapping out the steps to bring my vision to life.

By the time evening approaches, I've made significant progress. The skeleton of my business plan is more fleshed out, the path ahead clearer. But my mind keeps drifting back to Calvin, to Boris, and to the possible dangers we may be facing ahead.

I close my laptop for a break, taking a moment to look out the window, the trees swaying gently in the evening breeze. There's a sense of calm here, a tranquility that belies the storm we're navigating. I know that when I go downstairs, I'll have to face the reality of our situation again. But for now, in this moment, there's peace.

I stand, stretching my arms above my head, feeling the tension of the day melt away. Kiki, ever the faithful companion, purrs softly at my feet, a comforting presence. I take a deep breath, steeling myself for the conversation ahead with Ivan.

We have a lot to discuss.

CHAPTER 29

IVAN

"Fyodor, I'm fine," I assure my brother, my voice firm but weary. The weight of the situation presses heavily on me, but I can't afford to show any weakness, not now. Not even to my most trusted ally.

Fyodor studies me over his glass of whiskey, his expression skeptical. "You sure about that? You've been tense ever since Boris showed up. And pushing Julie away like that..." He trails off, his concern evident.

I let out a heavy sigh, running a hand through my hair. "I had to, Fyodor. Julie can focus on her non-profit, and it was the only way to ensure she'd be out of harm's way while we figure this out. She's safer thinking about that, rather than being caught up in all this mess with Boris."

Fyodor nods slowly, understanding my rationale. "I get it, but you can't keep her in the dark forever. She's a part of this now, like it or not."

"I know," I reply, my jaw setting with determination. "But for now, keeping her occupied with her project is the best option. We need to focus on handling Boris and the Bratva without dragging her into the line of fire."

Fyodor takes a sip of his coffee, his gaze piercing. "So, what's the plan? Boris is not going to back down easily. Are we considering moving away? Starting over somewhere else?"

I shake my head, my mind already forming a strategy. "No, we're not running. That's not how we handle things. I've got a plan. It's risky, but if it works, we can cut ties with the Bratva for good."

Fyodor leans forward, his interest piqued. "I'm all ears, brother. What are you thinking?"

"We need to turn the tables on Boris. Make him think he's got the upper hand, then hit him where it hurts. We use his own tactics against him."

Fyodor raises an eyebrow, his intrigue growing. "Sounds like you've got something specific in mind."

"I do," I confirm, my voice low.

"Well, don't keep me in suspense, Ivan. Give me the details." Fyodor leans forward with anticipation.

I walk over to the window, my hands clasped behind my back. Gazing out at the gently falling snow, I'm acutely aware of the gravity of what I'm about to undertake. This is more than a gamble; it's a move that will change the course of our lives, yet again.

"I've made some significant contacts through my company," I begin, enjoying the serene dance of the snowflakes outside. "One of them is Deputy Director Will Hargrove, second-in-command at the FBI. He's on our side and he'll be here within the hour."

Fyodor's eyes widen in surprise. "The FBI? That's a big card to play, one we usually stay away from. What do you think Hargrove will want in return?"

I turn from the window, meeting Fyodor's gaze with a steely resolve. "I have a pretty good idea," I admit with a heavy sigh. "They'll want information in exchange for their help, leverage against the Bratva. And I'm prepared to give it to them."

Fyodor leans back, absorbing the implications. "You're talking about turning informant? That's a dangerous path, Ivan."

"I know," I acknowledge, the weight of the decision making it hard to breathe. "But it's the only way to ensure Julie's safety, and to rid ourselves of Boris and his hold over us."

"And how exactly do you plan to do that?" Fyodor asks, a note of concern in his voice.

"I'll wear a wire," I reveal, the words tasting like a bitter pill. "We'll set up a meeting with Boris, make him believe I'm on board with his plan. I'll get him to admit to wanting to launder his illegally earned money through my gambling operations."

Fyodor nods slowly, the graveness of the situation etched on his face. "And the envelope Boris left, the one with the account numbers?"

"With that and the recorded confession, we'll have enough to bring him down. He won't see it coming."

Fyodor stands, pacing the room. "It's a bold move, Ivan. You're playing with fire. But if it means ending this nightmare, then I'm behind you."

I nod, feeling a sense of solidarity with my brother. "It's the only way we end this, Fyodor. We end this now, for Julie, for us, for our future."

Fyodor, leaning back in his chair, regards me with a mix of concern and skepticism. "You do realize the magnitude of the risk you're taking, right? What if Boris decides to pat you down and discovers the wire? You know they won't hesitate to kill you right there."

I nod, fully aware of the danger I'm placing myself in. "I've considered that. It's a calculated risk, but one we need to take."

He rubs his chin thoughtfully. "And even if you take Boris down, you know as well as I do there will be others to take his place. The Bratva is like a hydra; cut off one head, two more grow back."

"I know," I concede. "But we have to start somewhere. Boris' hold over us ends now. And that's why I need you here, Fyodor. Not just for your skills, but because of what Julie and I have been working on."

Fyodor raises an eyebrow. "Working on?"

I can't help but chuckle at his feigned innocence. "We're trying to start a family."

He laughs, a deep, hearty sound. "Ivan, it's okay to say you're having sex with your wife. I'm not going to blush."

"Shut up," I say, but there's a lightness in my voice, a brief respite from the grimness of our situation.

He becomes serious again, his gaze piercing. "Working with the FBI... that's a hell of a thing for a former Bratva member to do."

I meet his gaze squarely. "That's just it, Fyodor. I'm ready to sever ties with the Bratva, once and for all. No more half-measures, no more looking over my shoulder. I want a clean break, a fresh start. For Julie, for our future children, and for me."

Fyodor leans forward, placing his glass on the table. "It's a noble path you're choosing, Ivan. Dangerous, but noble. I'll be here, every step of the way. We'll face whatever comes together."

I nod, grateful for his support. "Thank you, brother. It means more than you know."

We sit in silence, the weight of the upcoming encounter with Boris and the FBI looming over us. It's a gamble, a play that could either free us from the shackles of our past or plunge us deeper into a world of danger and deceit.

Fyodor shifts uncomfortably in his chair, his brow furrowed in thought. "Ivan, I don't want to sound morbid, but have you considered, well, what if something happens to you?"

I nod solemnly, the magnitude of the situation not lost on me. "I've thought about it, Fyodor. And I've made arrangements, just in case."

He nods, his expression serious. "What kind of arrangements?"

"I've already had my lawyer draft my will. If something happens to me, you'll take over the company," I explain, watching his reaction closely.

Fyodor's eyes widen in surprise. "Me? Take over the company?"

"Yes," I affirm. "You're the only one I trust to handle it the right way. And more importantly," I pause, the thought of Julie weighing heavily on my heart, "I know you'll ensure that Julie is well taken care of. I want her to have everything she needs, for the rest of her life."

Fyodor runs a hand through his hair, visibly distressed by the conversation. "I hate this, Ivan. It feels like we're planning for your funeral."

I sigh, feeling the weight of his words. "I know, and I hate it too. But we have to be realistic. This situation with Boris and the Bratva is dangerous, and we can't pretend otherwise."

He nods reluctantly, the lines of his face etched with concern. "Alright. I'll do it, but only because I know it's what you want. Just promise me you'll do everything in your power to make sure you stay safe."

I offer him a grim smile. "You have my word, Fyodor. I plan to come out of this alive."

There's a pause as we both reflect on the enormity of what's at stake. Then, Fyodor breaks the silence. "What are you going to tell Julie when you head back to the city? You know she's going to want to stay with you. She won't just sit here while you put yourself in danger."

I exhale deeply, the thought of facing Julie and her reaction to my plan weighing heavily on me. "I honestly don't know yet. But one thing's for sure—it's going to be a fight. She's strong-willed, and she won't take kindly to being left behind, even if it's for her own safety."

Fyodor nods, understanding the predicament. "You're in a tough spot, brother. But whatever you do, don't lie to her. She deserves the truth, no matter how hard it might be."

I nod in agreement, knowing he's right. "I'll figure something out. But lying to her isn't an option. I respect her too much for that."

We sit in silence for a moment, each lost in our thoughts. The plan to work with the FBI and take down Boris is a gamble that puts everything on the line.

The vibration of my phone breaks the heavy stillness in the room, and I glance at the screen to see a text from Deputy Director Hargrove.

On my way.

My heart beats a little faster with anticipation and anxiety. This is it—the moment where everything either falls into place or unravels completely.

My brother, reading the distress on my face, stands up. "I need a moment," he says, his voice strained, "to wrap my head around all this."

I nod, understanding his need for space. "Take your time," I reply. He exits the room, leaving me alone with my thoughts, a maelstrom of emotions churning inside me.

Sitting back, I let out a long, weary sigh. How did I get here? Why did I ever get involved with the Bratva in the first place? I'm overcome by frustration for myself—each decision, each action and inaction of my past, feels like a chain linking me to a life I'm desperate to leave behind. A life that is threatening everything I hold dear. I feel as if there's a vice on my throat.

Compelled by a need to see my wife, I rise and quietly make my way upstairs. Peeking into the room where she is working, I pause at the doorway, watching her in silence. She's completely engrossed in her project, her focus and dedication evident in her every movement. She doesn't notice my presence, and I don't disturb her, content just to observe.

As I stand there, a surge of emotion washes over me. It's a feeling unlike anything I've ever experienced. It hits deeper, and it's more profound. It's not just love; it's a fierce, protective urge, a willingness to do anything, sacrifice anything for her safety and happiness.

Turning away from the door, I head back downstairs, my mind set on the task ahead. The meeting with Deputy Director Hargrove will set everything in motion. It's a risky plan that could either free me from my past or entangle me further, but I'm ready to face it head-on.

Julie and our future together are now my reason. For that, I'll confront my past, work with the FBI, and do whatever it takes to dismantle the shadow that's been looming over us. I've lived in the grey areas of morality for too long; it's time to step into the light and fight for the life I want, the life we deserve.

As I prepare for Hargrove's arrival, my resolve hardens. This is more than just a mission; it's a redemption, a chance to right the wrongs of my past and pave the way for a future filled with hope and love. No half-measures, no looking back.

CHAPTER 30

JULIE

The incessant buzzing of my phone shatters my concentration. I try to ignore it, but it's like a persistent mosquito, impossible to tune out. With a huff of irritation, I finally break away from my spreadsheet paradise and check the screen. Twelve texts, four voicemails, all from Calvin.

My stomach churns at the sight of his name. Just thinking about him, about the man responsible for so much pain and loss in my life, sends a wave of nausea through me. The barrage of messages feels invasive, a stark reminder of a past I've worked hard to distance myself from.

I sit there, phone in hand, debating what to do. Each notification feels like a weight, pulling me back to a place of anger and confusion. I've managed to build a life without him filled with love and purpose. And yet, here he is, trying to wedge himself back into my world.

With a deep breath, I swipe through the messages, not really reading them, just glimpsing enough to know they're all pleas for contact, for a chance to explain, to reconnect. The voicemails are likely more of the same. Part of me wants to delete them all, to block his number and pretend he doesn't exist. But another part, a small, curious part, wonders what he could possibly have to say that would make any difference now.

I set the phone down. My thoughts collide with the reality of my current situation, of Ivan's troubles with the Bratva, our unexpected retreat to this cabin for safety, the pregnancy I still haven't told Ivan about. It's like I'm juggling grenades, and my father's sudden reappearance is just another explosive in the mix.

Shaking my head, I try to refocus on my work, but it's no use. My zone has been broken, my mind now occupied with the ghosts of my past. I stand up, stretching my tense muscles, and walk over to the window. My mind keeps circling back to those unread texts and unheard voicemails. It's like a mental itch that won't go away, no matter how hard I try to ignore it.

With a frustrated sigh, I give in to the nagging urge. Picking up my phone, I hit the call button on my father's number.

"What the hell are you doing?" I demand the moment he picks up, not bothering to mask the irritation in my voice.

"Julie, I've been trying to get a hold of you for an hour," he says, his voice filled with both relief and urgency.

I roll my eyes, even though he can't see it. "Yeah, I know. I was ignoring you," I snap back, my patience thin. "I'm not ready to talk to you."

There's a pause on the other end, and when he speaks again, his tone is softer, more earnest. "I understand that, Julie. I really do. But I'm calling because it's important. It's about your aunt Barb."

The mention of Barb instantly grabs my attention, my annoyance giving way to concern. "What about her? What's happened?" I ask, my voice laced with worry.

He hesitates, and I can almost hear him grappling with the right words. "She's had some sort of an accident, Julie," he finally says, and those words hit me like a ton of bricks.

My blood runs cold, a chill that has nothing to do with the snow outside. Panic and fear take over, a tumultuous mixture that threatens to sweep me away.

"What? How? Is she okay?" The questions tumble out of me, each one laced with a growing dread.

"I don't know all the details," he admits.

Anger, worry, and confusion crash together in my head. Why is he the one giving me this news? Why him, of all people? But the urgency of the situation pushes those thoughts aside. Right now, Barb is all that matters.

My skepticism kicks into high gear as worry gnaws at me. "How do you even know about this?" I question sharply. "It's not like Barb would call you in an emergency situation. She hates your guts."

There's another brief pause on the other end, and when my father speaks again, his voice carries a hint of sheepishness. "I was at the deli down the block from her place. I was hoping you'd be visiting again and I could catch you," he admits.

I feel a surge of anger at his confession. "You mean you were stalking me? You do realize that's probably a violation of your probation, right?" I snap, my voice rising with each word.

"I know, I know, but I just wanted to see you, Julie," he rushes to explain. "But while I was there, an ambulance pulled up in front of Barb's house."

His words send a chill down my spine, but I'm still wary of believing him outright. "An ambulance?" I ask.

"Yeah," he confirms. "I watched as the EMTs loaded her into the back. I couldn't tell exactly what was wrong, but she didn't appear to be conscious."

The image he paints is enough to send a wave of panic through me. Barb, unconscious and being loaded into an ambulance is a scenario I'm not prepared for. My heart races, a mix of fear for my aunt and frustration at the situation.

"I have to go check on her," I stammer, my mind racing with what I need to do next.

"Julie, I'm sorry," my father's voice cuts in, sounding genuinely remorseful. "I know I'm the last person you want to hear from, but I thought you should know."

I barely register his words, my focus already shifting to Barb and her well-being. "I've got to go," I say quickly, ending the call without waiting for a response.

Frustration and worry twist inside me as I frantically dial Barb's number, each ring echoing in my ears like a ticking clock. When it goes to voicemail I leave a message, my voice strained with urgency. "Aunt Barb, it's Julie. Please call me back as soon as you get this. I'm worried about you."

As I'm about to redial, my phone lights up with an incoming call from my father. I decline it immediately, my fingers moving quickly to send Barb a text message. *Barb, please, I need to know that you're okay. Call me.*

No sooner have I hit send, Calvin tries calling again. This time, I answer with a sharp, "Stop calling me, I'm trying to get through to Barb!"

His voice, tinged with an annoying calmness, comes through. "Julie, she won't be able to answer. She's at the hospital." He tells me the name of the hospital before I can even respond.

I end the call and immediately dial the hospital's number, my fingers trembling slightly.

The conversation with the hospital staff is fruitless. They refuse to give out any information, citing privacy policies. My pleas fall on deaf ears, leaving me feeling helpless and even more anxious.

As I'm about to call Calvin back—something I never thought I'd consider—my phone rings. It's him again. I answer with a terse, "I called the hospital but I couldn't get anything out of them."

He hesitates before speaking. "Do you want me to meet you there? I can—"

"No," I cut him off sharply. "I don't need you. Just stay away from me." The last thing I need is him complicating things further.

I hang up, my mind racing. I need to get to the hospital to find out what's happened. As I head out, I realize I also need to inform Ivan. He needs to know where I am, especially with everything that's going on.

As I hurry downstairs, the cabin feels eerily quiet, almost as if it's holding its breath. "Ivan? Fyodor?" I call out, my voice echoing in the empty space. There's no response, just the sound of my own footsteps against the hardwood floor.

I reach for my phone to call Ivan, but as it dials, a distant ringing catches my ear. I follow the sound to the kitchen, finding his phone abandoned on the table, ringing with my call. A sense of urgency grips me. Where could he have gone without his phone?

Peering out the back window, I spot two guards patrolling the area. Their presence is somewhat reassuring, but it doesn't help my current dilemma.

I need to leave, now. Without a second thought, I quickly scribble a note to Ivan:

Ivan, I had to go. It's Barb, she's in the hospital. I couldn't reach you. I'll call as soon as I know more.

Julie

My hands are shaking as I leave the note on the table.

I grab my coat as I head out the door. The cold air hits me like a slap. I'm terrified, my thoughts a jumble of fear and worry. I'm not thinking straight, but I know that I need to get to Barb. She's always been there for me, and now it's my turn to be there for her.

I sneak around the guards' SUV, praying that they left the keys somewhere inside. Quietly, I open the door and hunch down, looking in the cup holders, under the visor, beneath the floor mat. I check the console and... yes! There they are.

As I start the car, I take a deep breath, trying to steady my racing heart. The engine roars to life, a steady rhythm in the midst of my turmoil. As I pull out of the driveway, the cabin and frantically running guards slowly disappear behind me, and I focus on the road ahead.

CHAPTER 31

IVAN

Deputy Director William Hargrove arrives at the cabin, his presence commanding and imposing. He's a tall, broad-shouldered man in his late fifties, with a stern, weathered face that speaks of years spent in the field. His eyes are sharp, scanning the surroundings with a practiced eye, missing nothing. His hair is a salt-and-pepper crew cut, and he moves with military precision.

"Deputy Director Hargrove," I greet him, extending a hand.

"Mr. Stepanov," he nods, shaking my hand with a firm grip. His gaze shifts to Fyodor briefly before settling back on me.

We convene in the basement, a space that feels both secure and isolated, perfect for the confidential nature of our meeting. The atmosphere is tense, charged with the significance of what we're about to discuss.

"Let's get straight to the point," Hargrove kicks it off. "This mission is high-risk. You need to be fully aware of what you're getting into."

I nod, my expression serious. "I understand the risks. I'm ready to do what's necessary to bring this asshole down."

Hargrove nods, pulling out a small device from his briefcase. "This is the latest in covert recording technology. It's virtually undetectable, but if Boris' men decide to pat you down, it could still be found, depending on how thorough they are. You need to be prepared for that possibility."

I take the device, examining it closely. It's smaller than I expected, no larger than a coin and looks like a tie pin. "Understood. What exactly do you need Boris to say to make the charges stick?"

"We need details about the money laundering operations," Hargrove explains. "Specifics about accounts, methods, any partners he's working with. And if he threatens you or discusses any other illegal activities, that's a bonus."

Fyodor interjects, "And if he suspects anything?"

Hargrove meets his gaze. "Then we move in immediately. But that's a last resort. We need this to be clean, by the book. We can't afford any mistakes."

I feel the weight of the responsibility settle on my shoulders. "I'll get you what you need," I say, determination steeling my voice.

Hargrove nods, his expression grim. "Remember, Ivan, your safety is paramount."

I look at Fyodor, then back at Hargrove. "I understand."

As Fyodor, Deputy Director Hargrove, and I step out of the basement, I can't help but feel a pang of unease at leaving Julie behind. I secured the cabin meticulously, ensuring that every possible measure of safety was in place, but worry for Julie's protection still lingers like a shadow.

"Let's get moving," Hargrove says. "I parked inconspicuously down the way, on the other side of the woods."

The evening is cool and overcast, the sky a uniform slate gray. Fyodor, walking beside me, wears a deep frown, his unease with the plan evident. "I don't like this, Ivan," he mutters, his voice low.

I nod, understanding his concerns. "Neither do I, but we don't have much choice."

The three of us make our way through the dense woods surrounding the cabin, our footsteps crunching into the thick carpet of fresh fallen snow. The conversation is intense, focused on the details of the plan to entrap Boris.

Suddenly, the distant sound of a car engine roaring to life breaks the natural stillness of the woods. My head snaps up, a frown forming as the meaning behind the unexpected noise registers. Something's not right. No one should be leaving until the next shift of guards arrives.

I instinctively reach for my phone, only to realize with a sinking feeling that I've left it back at the cabin. "Fyodor," I call out, my voice tense, "Call the guards. Now."

Fyodor quickly pulls out his phone, dialing the number with swift, precise movements. I turn back toward the cabin, my strides long and urgent. Deputy Director Hargrove's voice follows me. "Ivan, what's happening?"

"I'm not sure but it isn't good."

As we hasten back through the trees, Fyodor's voice cuts through the air, sharp and alarmed. "Ivan, it's Julie. She's taken off."

A cold dread washes over me, a fear like I've never known clutching at my chest. Without a second thought, I snatch the phone from Fyodor's hand. "What the fuck?" I bark into the receiver. "Why did you let her leave? Did she say where she's going?"

The guard on the other end stammers out a response, but it doesn't matter. Julie is out there, alone and exposed to the danger we've been trying so hard to shield her from. My mind races with possibilities, each more terrifying than the last.

I quicken my pace, practically running now. Hargrove and Fyodor are close behind, their footsteps heavy in the underbrush. The urgency of the situation is clear to all of us.

"Ivan, we need to stick to the plan," Hargrove insists, trying to keep his voice level despite the obvious emergency.

But my focus is on one thing and one thing only—Julie. Everything else fades into the background, insignificant compared to her safety. "The plan can wait," I snap back. "Julie is out there alone, and God knows what could happen to her."

I'm calculating my next move, the various scenarios playing out in my mind.

"Get your car," I order Fyodor, my voice commanding. "We need to find her before anyone else does."

Fyodor nods, a grim determination on his face as he hurries to comply. Hargrove follows, his expression tight with concern.

My grip tightens on the phone as I listen to the guard's explanation, a simmering rage building inside me with every word he utters. His voice, laced with a mixture of confusion and helplessness, does nothing to quell the storm brewing within me.

"So she just drove away?" I hiss into the phone, my tone sharp as a blade. "And you watched her leave?"

"We were following your orders, Mr. Stepanov. We were patrolling the grounds, maintaining the perimeter. We didn't expect—"

I cut him off, my voice rising in anger. "You're supposed to be protecting her! What's the point of you being here if you let her just drive off?"

There's a pause, the guard's voice faltering under the weight of my fury. "I'm sorry, sir. We didn't think she'd leave. By the time we realized what was happening, it was too late."

"Follow her, now!" I bark into the phone. "Get in your car and track her down."

Another pause, the guard's next words fueling my anger further. "She took our vehicle, Mr. Stepanov. We don't have a way to follow her."

"Save it," I interrupt, my voice cold with disgust and exasperation. "What kind of security detail leaves their keys unattended? You're fired. Both of you."

Fyodor glances at me, his expression one of concern. "Ivan, we'll find her. She can't have gone far."

My feet pound against the ground as I run, every muscle tensed and ready for action. Fyodor and Deputy Director Hargrove are close on my heels, their breaths echoing in the quiet.

I burst through the front door, my mind racing with scenarios and possibilities. Where could Julie have gone?

I snatch my phone from the kitchen table, dialing Julie's number with shaking fingers. I hear the ring in my ear as well as across the room from where her phone sits on the counter.

Panic grips me, a tight knot in my stomach. Julie's disappearance is out of character, not to mention alarming. She's well aware of the danger and understands the precarious situation we're in. For her to leave so abruptly and without her phone, it has to be something critical.

I turn to Deputy Director Hargrove, my decision made. "I know we have a deal, but I have to go after her," I say, the words rushed, desperate.

Understanding flashes in Hargrove's eyes, a nod of acknowledgment. "Go. We'll be in touch," he says, his voice firm.

Fyodor tosses me the car keys, but then stops dead in his tracks. "Look at this," he says, holding up a piece of paper. I rush over, my eyes frantically scanning the words that have been scribbled across the page.

"Let's go."

We run outside to the car and I slip into the driver's seat, my hands gripping the steering wheel.

"We'll catch up to her," Fyodor assures me, his voice calm though I can hear the underlying concern.

I nod as I turn my attention on the road ahead. Julie's safety is my only concern now. The car roars to life, and I tap the accelerator, the engine responding with a powerful surge.

We speed down the driveway, the trees a blur as we make our way onto the main road. Every second feels like an eternity, each minute stretching out with the weight of my worry for Julie.

Fyodor checks his phone, trying to reach the guards, gather any information he can. "They said she left in a hurry, didn't say a word to anyone," he reports, his voice tight.

I grit my teeth, frustration and fear battling within me. What could have driven her to take such a risk? The only answer that makes sense is Barb, her aunt, the one person she'd go to any lengths for.

The car speeds along the highway, cutting through the landscape as we follow the route to the city.

CHAPTER 32

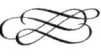

JULIE

Twenty minutes into the drive, I reach for my phone to call Barb again, only to realize with a sinking feeling that it's not there. I must have left it back at the cabin in my rush to get out of there. *Shit.*

For a brief moment I consider turning back, but that would only delay me further. If Barb really is in the hospital, I need to get to her, and fast.

I grip the steering wheel tighter, my mind racing as I navigate the familiar route back to the city. The road unwinds before me, a path I'd thankfully paid close attention to during our drive out to the cabin. Now, each turn and landmark guides me back.

As I drive, my thoughts turn to my father and his sudden reappearance in my life. Would he lie about something as serious as Barb being in the hospital? It doesn't add up. Yet there's a nagging voice in the back of my mind, a suspicion that he's playing some sort of game. His eagerness to see me, to forge a connection after all these years, it just feels off. It's not the warm, fatherly concern one would expect, but something more calculated, more self-serving.

I shake my head, trying to clear it of such troubling thoughts. Right now, my focus has to be on Barb. She's been the one constant in my life, the rock I've always been able to lean on. The thought of her being hurt, possibly sick, sends a wave of fear through me.

I push down on the accelerator a little more, the New York skyline slowly coming into view. The familiar streets and buildings offer a small sense of comfort, a reminder of the life I've built here. But under the surface, there's a current of unease, of uncertainty about what I'm heading into.

As I enter into the city, the traffic thickens, the pace of life picking up around me. I weave through the streets, my determination growing with each mile that brings me closer to Barb's place. I decide to go there first, just in case my father was lying.

The city's rhythm engulfs me as I make my way toward Barb's building. I'm moving quickly, my thoughts filled with worry and doubt. The drive took less time than I expected, but then again, I wasn't exactly mindful of the speed limits.

I park the car a block away from Barb's building and as soon as I step out I hear my name called. Turning, I see Calvin hurrying toward me. My frown deepens instinctively. I keep walking, but he catches up to me, breathless.

"I knew you'd come," he says, a hint of triumph in his voice that sets my nerves on edge.

I don't like the way he says it, as if he's orchestrated this whole scenario. "Did you really see Barb being put into an ambulance?" I ask, skepticism lacing my tone.

He hesitates, and then his expression shifts. "No, I didn't. As far as I know, she's fine. But I have a friend who needs to speak with you and this was the only thing I could think of that would get you to come."

I stop in my tracks, a cold feeling settling in the pit of my stomach. "What are you talking about?" My voice is sharp, my patience wearing thin. "You lied to me. Why the hell should I believe anything you say now?"

His eyes dart around nervously, and he leans in closer, lowering his voice. "I know it's a lot to ask after everything. But this is important, Julie. Please, just hear me out."

I take a step back, distancing myself from him. "You can't just lie to me about something like that and expect me to go along with whatever you're planning. What's this really about?"

He looks around again, clearly uneasy, then focuses back on me. "It's about your safety, Julie. There are things you don't know, things that could put you in danger."

His words send a chill down my spine, and a thousand questions flood my mind. "What do you mean, my safety? What danger?"

He glances over his shoulder, then back at me. "I can't say anything more here. It's not safe. But if you come with me, I can explain everything."

I'm torn; my instincts screaming at me to walk away, to find Barb and forget this man and his cryptic warnings. But a part of me driven by anger and curiosity, wants to know what he's talking about.

After a moment of internal struggle, I make my decision. "Fine. I'll hear what you have to say. But no games. If you're lying to me again, I'm done. Understood?"

He nods eagerly, relief washing over his face. "Understood, Julie. Thank you."

I begin to follow him but my steps soon falter as I catch sight of the Bratva boss and two of his menacing associates lingering near a nondescript van. My heart sinks as I realize this is a setup, a trap, and I've walked right into it.

I instinctively try to turn back, to make a dash for the car, but my father's hand clamps down on my arm, holding me in place. "Just hear them out, Julie," he urges, his voice a mix of desperation and deceit.

I jerk my arm away, my voice rising in alarm. "How do you know those men?"

His eyes dart toward Boris and his goons, then back at me. "Listen, I can help you get out of this. But you have to help me, too."

I stare at him, disbelief and anger swirling inside me. "Help you how?" I demand, my voice laced with suspicion.

He leans in, his voice a hushed whisper. "I need money, Julie. Your new husband's rich, right? Help me get some cash, and I'll get you out of this mess."

I feel like I've been punched in the stomach. The realization that my father orchestrated this, that he's using me as a pawn in his desperate game for money, is sickening.

"You set me up?" I hiss, my voice trembling with rage and fear.

"I did, but I can fix this," he insists, a wild look in his eyes. "Just promise me the money, and we'll get away from these guys."

I shake my head, disgust and horror filling me. "You think Ivan would give you a dime? You're delusional! And these men, the Bratva? They won't hesitate to kill you once they're done using you."

His face falls, his scheme unraveling before him. "Julie, please. I need this. I don't have anywhere else to go."

I take a step back, my mind racing. I need to get away, to escape this nightmare. "You're on your own, Calvin. I can't help you, and I won't. Not after this."

I turn to leave but the sound of heavy footsteps makes my blood run cold. The Bratva men are approaching, their intentions clear in their cold, calculating eyes.

My father reaches out, a last-ditch effort to hold me back. "Julie, wait! Please!"

But I'm already moving, adrenaline coursing through my veins. I have to get away, to warn Ivan, to protect myself and the life growing inside me. Calvin's betrayal, the danger he's put me in, it's unforgivable.

Boris' men catch up to me. One of them roughly shoves Calvin to the ground, while the other clamps a hand over my mouth, silencing any attempt to scream. His grip is iron-tight and unyielding. Panic-stricken, I thrash and kick, trying to break free from his grasp.

My father's voice, filled with fear and anger, cuts through the chaos. "We had a deal! What are you doing?" His protest is desperate, the words of a man realizing too late that he's out of his depth.

Amidst my struggle, a strange, muffled pop echoes through the air, followed by Calvin's agonized scream. My heart pounds in terror, the reality of the situation hitting me with brutal clarity. This is no longer just a threat; it's a nightmare unfolding in real time.

Before I can process what's happening, I'm being dragged toward the van. I kick and squirm, but the men are too strong, their hold on me unbreakable. A gag is forced into my mouth, stifling my cries, and a bag is pulled over my head, plunging me into darkness.

I feel the cold metal of handcuffs snapping around my wrists, binding me helplessly. My mind races with fear and desperation. This can't be happening. I can't let them take me, I have to get back to Ivan. But the more I struggle, the tighter their grip becomes.

The van's door slams shut, sealing me inside with my captors. I hear the engine start, and we begin moving. Every turn and bump in the road sends a fresh wave of fear through me.

As the van speeds away, I'm left alone with my fear, the darkness of the bag suffocating, the handcuffs a cold reminder of my helplessness. My mind clings to the hope that Ivan will find me, that he'll come to my rescue. He has to. I can't face this alone. Not with so much at stake.

CHAPTER 33

IVAN

I'm pushing the car to its limits, my hands gripping the steering wheel tight as I navigate through the congested streets of Manhattan. Every second counts, and my mind fills with worst-case scenarios. Julie is out here alone, and every fiber of my being is screaming to find her.

Fyodor's beside me, his expression grim, a mirror of my own concern. He points out the guards' SUV as we approach Barb's building. Julie isn't in it. My heart sinks. I know something's wrong.

I slam the car into park and bolt out, rushing toward the building with a singular focus. Director Hargrove's information, the address he had provided, echoes in my mind. This has to lead somewhere.

A crowd has formed nearby, and my instincts tell me it's not for anything good. I force my way through, elbows out, my presence demanding space. People turn, their expressions a mix of shock and curiosity, but I don't have time for politeness. I need answers.

At the center of the crowd, I find a man lying on the ground, his body twisted in an unnatural way. Blood pools around him, painting the pavement red. He's a stranger to me, not anyone I recognize, but the violence of the scene tells me this is no ordinary shooting.

I scan the crowd, searching for any sign of Julie or someone who might have seen something. My mind races with questions.

The wounded man is barely conscious, his breathing ragged and shallow. I crouch beside him, my training kicking in. "Hey, can you hear me?" I ask, my voice steady despite the turmoil inside.

He groans, his eyes fluttering open for a moment. There's fear in his gaze, a haunted look that speaks of horrific things seen and done. "Help," he rasps, his voice barely audible.

I glance up at Fyodor, who's already on his phone, calling for an ambulance. "We need to find out what happened here," I say to Fyodor before turning back to the man. "Did you see a woman? Blonde hair, about this tall?" I gesture with my hand, the image of Julie clear in my mind.

The man's eyes widen slightly, recognition flickering in their depths. "Ambush," he coughs, the word laced with pain. "Took her... van."

My heart stops for a moment. *Took her*. He must mean Julie. The pieces click into place, forming a picture I'd been dreading. She's been taken, and this man, whoever he is, witnessed it.

"*Who* took her? Do you know where?" I press, urgency sharpening my words.

The man shakes his head weakly, blood trickling from the corner of his mouth. "Didn't see... faces..."

The ambulance's siren wails in the distance, growing louder each second. I stand up, frustration and fear battling within me. Julie is out there, in the hands of unknown enemies, and I'm clueless about where to start looking.

As the paramedics arrive and begin tending to the man, I step back, my mind working overtime. This was no random attack—it's connected to Boris, to the Bratva, to the danger we've been trying to escape.

"Ivan," Fyodor says, his voice low. "We need to regroup. Think this through."

I nod, my jaw clenched. He's right. Charging in blindly won't help Julie. I need a plan, a way to find her quickly and bring her back safely.

I listen in as the paramedics ask the man his name. He says it's Calvin. As the paramedics load him onto a stretcher, he reaches an arm out toward me to beckon me closer. He tells me he is Julie's father and a new heaviness descends on the situation. Calvin's face is twisted in pain, but there's a glimmer of something else in his eyes, fear, maybe even regret. "I asked Julie to meet me here, at Barb's place," he gasps, wincing with every word. "But she never made it to the door. Three men grabbed her, just snatched her right off the street and threw her into a van."

My hands clench into fists, the fury building inside of me like a storm. "Which way did they go? Did you see the van's license plate?" I press, trying to keep my voice level.

Calvin shakes his head, coughing slightly. "I couldn't see... they were fast. One of them shot me when I tried to stop them," he says.

Fyodor chimes in. "Did you recognize any of them? Anything that could help us find them?"

Calvin closes his eyes for a moment, gathering his strength. "No, I didn't recognize them. But one of them... he had a tattoo, right here," he points to his neck, "some kind of symbol, looked like a... like a snake or dragon."

My mind races, processing this new information. A tattoo could be a lead, a way to identify at least one of the kidnappers. "Anything else? Any detail could help us," I ask, trying to piece together a plan of action.

Calvin looks up at me, his gaze meeting mine. "I'm sorry, I didn't... I just wanted to talk to her. I never thought..." His voice trails off, choked with emotion.

I take a deep breath, pushing back the rage and fear clawing at my insides. Julie is out there somewhere, in the hands of these men, and every second counts. "We need to move, Fyodor," I say, my voice steady but urgent. "We have to find her."

Fyodor nods, his eyes dark with determination. "Let's go. We'll start with the tattoo lead. And I'll make some calls, see if any of my contacts know anything."

As we turn to leave, I cast one last glance at Calvin lying there, a broken man whose actions have inadvertently endangered my wife. The complexity of the situation, the intertwining of past and present, it's all a tangled web that's tightening around us.

The truth suddenly hits me like a punch to the gut—Boris has Julie. Everything else, the complexities of her father's story, the reasons behind his appearance here, they all fall away in the realization. Julie is in the hands of that merciless man, and every second she remains with him, the amount of danger she's in grows.

As police sirens wail closer, Fyodor's words snap me back to the present. "We need to get out of here, Ivan. The cops will only slow us down," he urges, his voice tense.

He's right. We can't afford to be held up by police questioning, not now. We move swiftly to the car, , my mind already formulating our next steps. But as I slide into the driver's seat and reach for my phone, I'm stopped cold by a notification from an unknown number. My heart thunders in my chest as I open the message.

The image on the screen is a nightmare come to life, a scene from a classic horror movie. A woman lays helplessly in the back of a van, handcuffed, her head covered by a hood. Even without seeing her face, I know it's Julie. The fear that grips me is a cold, paralyzing terror that threatens to overwhelm every fiber of my being.

Fyodor leans over, his eyes widening as he sees the picture. "Jesus, Ivan, we have to find her. Now."

I nod, my jaw twitching. This goes beyond a kidnapping; it's a direct defiance, a brutal message from Boris. But he's made a critical mistake. By threatening Julie, causing her physical and mental discomfort, he's unleashed a fury in me that knows no bounds.

"We're going to find her, Fyodor. And when we do, Boris will regret ever crossing me."

HIS DEMANDS | 215

Fyodor doesn't argue. He knows as well as I do that this is no longer just a matter of outmaneuvering a criminal mastermind. This is personal.

The phone in my hand feels like a lifeline and a curse at the same time. Boris has sent me a reminder of the power he currently wields over Julie's fate. His number flashes on the screen, and with a deep breath to steel myself, I answer.

"Ivan," Boris' voice is taunting, oozing with malicious satisfaction. "I've decided your lovely wife will be staying with me for a while. At least until you've completed the task I've set for you."

Rage ignites within me, a searing inferno that threatens to consume my composure. "If you hurt her, Boris, I swear I'll kill you," I hiss, struggling to keep my voice steady.

Boris' laughter is a chilling sound, devoid of any humanity. "Oh, Ivan, such threats! But let me be clear—if you don't do exactly as I say, Julie will suffer. And I won't make it quick."

His words are a cold blade twisting in my gut. I know he's capable of unspeakable cruelty, but I can't let my fear for Julie cloud my judgment. I have to play along, buy time to find her.

"What do you want me to do?" I ask, each word tasting like bile.

Boris' tone turns businesslike, but the underlying menace never wavers. "It's simple. You have three days to launder a substantial sum through your company. Failure to comply will have dire consequences for your wife."

"I'm not doing anything until I speak to Julie," I demand, clinging to the slim hope of hearing her voice, confirming she's still alive.

There's a pause then an inaudible exchange before Boris barks an order. Julie's voice, full of fear and desperation, pierces the line. "Ivan!" she cries out, but her words are quickly stifled, a muffled sound replacing her plea.

"Enough! Get to work, Stepanov," Boris snaps before the line goes dead, leaving me in a deafening silence that echoes with Julie's scream.

The world spins around me.

Fyodor, who's been silently listening, places a hand on my shoulder. "We'll find her, Ivan. No matter what it takes," he says, his voice firm.

I nod, my determination reinforced tenfold. "We will. And Boris will pay for every second she's in his hands."

The urgency in my voice is palpable as I call Deputy Director Hargrove. "Boris has taken Julie. He's holding her hostage," I explain tersely, trying to keep my emotions in check. "One of his men shot her father. He's demanding I launder money for him."

"We'll start tracking them immediately, Ivan. But these things take time."

"Time is exactly what we don't have, Hargrove," I snap, the image of Julie, frightened and in danger, fueling my impatience. "I need her location, and I need it now." Without waiting for a response, I end the call.

Turning to Fyodor, I see the same determination in his eyes that I feel burning within myself. "I know some of Boris' usual hideouts. It's a long shot, but we have to start somewhere."

Fyodor nods, his expression apathetic. "Let's go then. We're not leaving her in that bastard's hands any longer than necessary."

CHAPTER 34

JULIE

An explosion of anger and anxiety overtakes me as I lay in the back of the van. The blindfold over my eyes envelopes me into darkness, ropes now binding my wrists replacing the handcuffs. Boris' goons also tied my ankles, making me feel even more vulnerable and helpless.

I can't believe I fell for Calvin's trap. The thought that he went so far as to lying about Barb being in danger stings, but what hurts even more is knowing I walked right into his scheme. I should have been more cautious, more skeptical. But the possibility of Barb being hurt blinded me to the risks.

I'm angry at Calvin, of course, but I'm even more furious with myself. I let my emotions get the better of me, rushing off without a second thought. And the worst part? I left my phone behind. Ivan can't track me, making it more difficult to find me quickly. It's a rookie mistake, and now I'm paying for it.

Alone with my thoughts, I try to wrap my head around everything. Ivan must be out of his mind with worry by now. I curse myself for not thinking things through, for putting myself and ultimately him in this dire situation.

The van has been moving for what feels like an eternity, jostling me around with every turn and bump in the road. The lack of vision is disorienting, making the passage of time feel even more drawn out. My mind races with possible scenarios of what awaits me, none of them calming.

Finally, the van comes to a halt. The back doors swing open, and a rush of cool air hits me, a stark contrast to the stuffy interior I've been confined in. Rough hands grip my arms, pulling me out of the van with little regard for my comfort. I wince, biting back a cry of pain as my knees hit the hard ground.

Something primal and fierce surges within me as hands grasp my arms again. I'm not going to let them take me without a fight. My body coils, every muscle tensing as I prepare to strike. My heart is racing, adrenaline pumping through my veins like determined fuel.

With a burst of energy, I lash out, my leg shooting up in a swift, powerful arc. I can feel the contact, the solid thud of my foot connecting with the assailant's chest. The satisfaction of landing a solid blow courses through me, a fleeting triumph.

Almost immediately, a crushing force slams into the side of my head. The impact is staggering, a brutal, blinding pain that radiates through my skull. It feels like my brain has been jolted, my senses thrown into chaos.

The sudden sharp pain that explodes in my head is like nothing I've ever experienced. It's a searing, blinding agony that sends my senses reeling. I've never been struck before, and the shock of it is almost as bad as the pain. The world tilts and spins, a dizzying rotation of light and shadow.

I'm reeling, fighting to stay conscious, refusing to give in to the darkness that threatens to engulf me. My head throbs with every beat of my heart, a relentless drumming that makes it hard to think, hard to focus. But I know I can't afford to pass out. I need to stay alert, need to be ready for any chance I get to escape or fight back.

Despite the pain, a part of me is fiercely proud of the blow I managed to land. It might have been a short-lived victory, but it still feels significant.

Lifted roughly to my feet, I'm disoriented and stumbling, my balance thrown off by the blindfold and the blow to my head. Every step is a precarious dance, a struggle to stay upright. The fabric over my eyes feels suffocating, a barrier not just to my vision but to my understanding of everything happening around me.

Determination surges within me, and I manage to work the gag out of my mouth with a defiant spit. My voice rings out, raw and loud, screaming for help.

"Help! Somebody help me!" I scream at the top of my lungs, my voice echoing with terror and urgency. "Please, anyone! Help!"

I continue to shout. "I'm being kidnapped! Please, help me!"

But my cries for help are met with a brutal response. A hard strike lands on the side of my face, a force so sudden and intense that it knocks the breath out of me. Pain explodes through my jaw, a deep, wrenching agony that causes me to double over. I want to keep screaming, to keep fighting, but the pain is too much.

"Hush up, you little bitch."

My hand instinctively goes to my stomach, a protective gesture for the precious life growing inside me. I have to protect this baby, no matter what. I can't risk another blow like that, there's no telling what it could do to my unborn child.

My screams die in my throat, replaced by a silent, steely resolve. Every instinct in me shifts to preservation, to shielding the tiny, fragile being depending on me.

As the blindfold is abruptly yanked off, my eyes take a moment to adjust to the dim lighting. I find myself in an environment I didn't expect, a deserted strip club. It's a bare, eerie place, devoid of any club-goers, waitstaff, and dancers.

The club has three stages, each with its own pole standing tall. The space feels haunted, a shadow of its usual vibrant self. The air is thick with the distinct smell of cheap perfume mixed with the lingering scent of sex, a combination that makes me cringe internally. The whole ambiance of the place is unsettling, a blunt reminder of the predicament I'm in.

Every surface seems to hold memories of countless nights, and there's a part of me that recoils at the thought of touching anything. The floors are sticky underfoot, and the chairs around the stages are haphazardly arranged, as if left in a hurry.

Settling uncomfortably onto a couch that reeks of alcohol and bad decisions, I grimace, trying to find a spot that feels less disgusting. It's like being on the set of a sleazy movie, and all I can think about is taking a long shower. I glance warily at Boris sitting across from me with an air of smug assurance.

"So, what's the big plan?" I ask, injecting a hint of sarcasm into my voice in an attempt to hide the terror I feel. "Ivan runs an errand for you, and I get a free pass out of this charming establishment?"

Boris chuckles, a sound that grates on my nerves. "It's simple. Ivan follows the instructions I gave him, and you're free to go."

I snort, unable to help myself. "Ivan doesn't do dirty work anymore. You've got the wrong guy."

His laugh this time is more of a scoff. "You'd be surprised what a man will do for the woman he loves."

I roll my eyes, trying to mask the unease his words stir in me. "Love's great and all, but it doesn't turn a legit businessman into a criminal overnight."

He leans back, eyeing me with amusement mixed with something darker. "You clearly underestimate what people are willing to do under pressure. Ivan will come around; they always do."

I shake my head, crossing my arms defiantly. "Well, I'm afraid you're in for a disappointment. Ivan's a lot of things, but he's no puppet on a string."

He smirks, clearly enjoying this little game. "We'll see, Mrs. Stepanov. We'll see."

I sit there, trying to appear nonchalant, but my thoughts are of Ivan, our baby, and the fear of what could come next. But I'm not about to give Boris the satisfaction of seeing me sweat.

His earlier statement—that Ivan would do anything for me—echoes in my head. It sends a thrill through me, despite the grimy, unsettling surroundings. But I tamper down the flutter in my heart, refusing to give him the satisfaction of knowing that anything he says has any sort of effect on me.

I turn my gaze away, staring at the gaudy neon lights of the club.

I wrap my arms protectively around myself, thinking of the baby and how much I wish I'd told Ivan about it. The thought of him not knowing and facing so much danger without the knowledge that he's going to be a father gnaws at me. So I make a silent vow to myself: as soon as I get out of this, as soon as I see Ivan again, I'm going to tell him.

After what feels like an eternity but is probably more like half an hour, I decide to make my move. I can't sit here passively, not when every second counts, not when there's a chance, however slim, that I could find a way out of this. The door to the bathroom catches my eye, a potential route to escape or at least to gather more information.

Trying to appear casual, I slowly stand up then perform a dramatic stretch. One of the men, startled out of his growing complacency, lurches to his feet, his eyes narrowing in suspicion. I roll my eyes at him, injecting as much disdain into my gesture as I can muster. Inside, my stomach is a chaotic flutter of nerves and fear, but I force myself to maintain a facade of confidence.

"I need to use the bathroom," I tell him.

To my relief they relent, albeit grudgingly. One of them nods toward the bathroom door, and I walk to it, my steps measured and deliberate. As I pass the door to the backstage area, I steal a glance, my mind racing with possibilities. There's got to be a back door, an exit they use for deliveries or emergencies.

The bathroom, a cramped space with flickering fluorescent lights, offers no escape. No windows, no hidden doors, just stark walls and a mirror revealing the tension and fear in my expression. I close the door partially behind me and peek through the crack, scanning the main room. The men seem relaxed, their attention diverted. It's now or never.

I quietly slip out of the bathroom, my heart pounding in my chest. The backstage area is just a few steps away. If I can sneak in there maybe I can find a way out. The musty smell of the club is stronger here, a mixture of perfume, stale smoke, and alcohol. I move as silently as I can, every sense heightened, every nerve on edge.

But luck isn't on my side. One of the men is sharper than the others and catches a glimpse of me attempting to sneak into the backstage area. His shout of alarm slices through the heavy air, and my instinctive reaction is to run. Adrenaline surges through me, fueling a desperate sprint toward what I hope is freedom.

The backstage area is a labyrinth of shadows and curtains, a confusing maze to someone unfamiliar with its layout. I can hear heavy footsteps behind me, closing in fast. Panic sets in; I'm running blindly, turning corners without thought, prey trying to outmaneuver its predator in unfamiliar territory.

He catches me easily, his grip like a vice around my arm. I struggle, trying to wrench myself free, but it's useless. He's too strong, too fast. I'm dragged back to the main room, my hope of escape crushed under the weight of his hold.

Boris looks at me, his expression a mix of disappointment and something darker, more menacing. His eyes are cold, calculating, and I feel a shiver run down my spine. There's a sense of danger about him that goes beyond physical threat, a psychological edge that makes him even more frightening.

"Where exactly did you think you were going, little girl?" he asks, his voice low and dangerous.

I muster as much defiance as I can, despite the fear gripping me. "Trying to get away from you," I snap back, meeting his cold stare head-on.

He chuckles dryly, a sound devoid of any actual humor. "There's nowhere to run. You're in over your head, sweetheart."

I glare at him, struggling against the iron grip of the man holding me. "Let me go! You won't get away with this."

His smirk widens. "Oh, but we already are. Your little escape attempt? Just a minor inconvenience. You should realize by now, there's no getting away from us."

He nods at the man holding onto my arm, a silent command that sends a wave of dread through me. Before I can react, I feel a sharp blow to the back of my head. The world spins, pain exploding in a bright flash of light. My legs buckle, and darkness rushes in to claim me. The last thing I feel is the hard floor rushing up to meet me as I fall into unconsciousness.

CHAPTER 35

IVAN

In the dimly lit study of my brownstone, Fyodor and I are poring over a map of the city, our fingers tracing potential hideouts where Boris could be holding Julie. Each location we consider seems less likely than the last. My gut tells me we are looking in the wrong places.

Fyodor leans back in his chair, a frown on his face. "None of these spots fit Boris' style."

I nod, frustration gnawing at me. "He's not following his usual pattern though. He's being unpredictable, trying to throw us off, and that makes him more dangerous."

Fyodor's gaze sharpens. "Are you even considering that job Boris asked you to do? Just to get Julie back safely?"

I shake my head vehemently. "Hell no. If I give in it'll prove that he's in control. I can't let that happen."

Fyodor sighs, running a hand through his hair. "But Julie's in severe danger, Ivan. We need to think about her safety."

"I am thinking about her safety," I snap, my worry for Julie fueling my anger. "But doing Boris' bidding isn't the solution. It's a temporary fix that will only lead to more demands, more control. I need to sever ties with the Bratva once and for all."

Fyodor leans forward, his eyes searching mine. "You know the risks involved, Ivan. You're putting a lot on the line."

"I know," I reply, my voice firm. "But I've been running from my past for too long. It's time to face it head-on. It's the only way to keep Julie safe going forward."

The room falls silent. Fyodor nods slowly, understanding where I'm coming from. "Alright. Let's do this."

I stand up, a newfound determination setting in. "We'll find her, Fyodor, and when we do, Boris will regret ever crossing me."

Fyodor stands beside me, a solid presence by my side. "I'm with you, brother. Let's bring her home."

The phone's shrill ring cuts through our tense deliberations. I grab it, hoping for a lead, any lead. It's Deputy Director Hargrove on the line. His voice is terse, efficient as always. I put him on speaker. "Boris, we've compiled a list of more potential locations. One of them stands out—an old strip club in the Bronx. We've got eyes in the area that saw a van pull up there not too long ago."

Fyodor leans in, his interest piqued. "Where in the Bronx?" he asks, scanning the map.

Hargrove gives the coordinates. "It's in a rundown area, seems secluded enough for Boris' purposes."

I end the call and we gather our gear along with the map. We hop into my SUV and every fiber of my being is taut with fear as we speed through the streets. Knowing Julie is in Boris' evil hands is unbearable. I know what he's capable of and I can't allow my thoughts to go to the unimaginable. It's far beyond just saving her now; it's reclaiming a future that's suddenly become essential to me.

"Fyodor, there's a gun in the glove compartment."

My brother's eyes widen in surprise as he pulls the weapon out. "I thought you were done with this, Ivan. When you started your company, I thought..."

"Extenuating circumstances," I cut him off, my gaze fixed on the road ahead. "I left that life behind, but it seems it's not quite done with me."

He weighs the gun in his hand, a silent acknowledgment of the seriousness of our mission. I can sense the concern, the anxiety he's feeling. But now's not the time for doubt or fear. Now's the time for action.

"We'll do whatever it takes," I say, my resolve ironclad. "I'm not losing Julie. Not now, not ever."

"I'm ready to do this brother," Fyodor says, his voice firm, echoing my determination.

"Good. We go in, we get her out. No heroics, just precision and speed," I instruct, my mind clear and focused. "And Fyodor, remember to stay close."

As we pull into the parking lot of the club—a rundown structure with a facade as uninviting as its reputation—my eyes are immediately drawn to the lone vehicle parked outside. A nondescript, white van but it stands out like a beacon of suspicion. It matches Calvin's description, and I know in my gut this is it. This is where they've taken Julie.

I scan the area, expecting to see Hargrove's men standing discreetly by, but there's no sign of the FBI. Only us and the ominous presence of the van. The lack of backup sets my nerves on edge, but it also sharpens my resolve. We're on our own, and every decision carries the weight of life and death.

"Fyodor, stay sharp," I say, my voice low.

Fyodor nods, his expression tight with concentration. He understands the stakes as well as I do. This isn't just a rescue mission; it's a personal crusade to save the woman I love.

I take a moment to assess the situation. The club itself is a fortress, no windows, no easy way to see what's happening inside. The front door appears to be our only point of entry, but it's also the most dangerous. It's likely guarded, and we have no idea what we're walking into.

"We need to be smart about this," I murmur, my brain ticking through the options. "Going in blind is too risky. We need a distraction, something to draw them out."

Fyodor's eyes meet mine, understanding flashing in them. "I can create a diversion," he offers. "Get them to open the door, give you a chance to slip in."

I consider his proposal. It's too risky, and I don't like it. "Let's see if there is another way in first. We don't know how many are inside, or what types of weapons they have. If we can sneak up on them from behind we might have a shot."

He gives a curt nod, determination etched on his features. "I agree. Our chances of overpowering them are better if they don't know we're coming."

I take a deep breath, trying to steady my nerves. The next few minutes will determine everything. We can't afford any mistakes. For Julie, for us, this has to be perfect.

CHAPTER 36

JULIE

Boris' face is contorted with fury as drags me into what can only be described as the dingiest room in this already seedy club. It's small, filthy, and reeks of stale smoke and sweat. He pushes me down onto a rickety chair and starts tying my wrists behind my back. The ropes bite into my skin, but I refuse to give him the satisfaction of seeing me wince.

"Let me go, you asshole!" I snap, my voice laced with venom. "Do you really think this is going to end well for you?"

He just smirks, a twisted grin that makes my skin crawl. "You're quite feisty, aren't you? But it won't do you any good. If your husband fails to do what we want, you'll be coming back to Russia with me. I could fetch a good price for a sassy blonde back home."

I snort, despite the fear curling in my stomach. "I'd chew through your neck before I let that happen."

His eyes narrow, and I can tell my words have hit a nerve. "You should be careful, little girl. You're not in a position to make threats."

I glare at him, my anger flaring. "My husband will tear you apart for this."

He laughs, a sound that's as unpleasant as his presence. "Your husband? He's going to be too busy trying to save his own skin. And if he fails, well..." His gaze rakes over me, making my skin crawl. "I have plans for you."

I want to spit in his face, to fight and scream, but I know it won't help. Instead, I force myself to calm down, to think. Ivan is out there, and he'll come for me. He has to.

Boris leaves, locking the door behind him, and I'm alone in the dim, filthy room. I test the ropes but they're tight, unyielding. I'm stuck, at least for now.

The silence allows my mind to go in ten different directions. *Ivan, where are you? What are you doing? You have to come for me. We have a future to think about, a baby to raise.* I can't let this be the end. I won't.

My thoughts focus on the baby growing inside me, and a fierce determination takes root. I have to protect him or her, I have to survive this nightmare. I close my eyes, focusing on the little life growing inside me, allowing it to be my strength now, my reason to keep fighting.

I start to wriggle, trying to loosen the ropes binding my wrists. I twist and turn, ignoring the sting and burn against my skin. After what feels like an eternity, I feel the ropes give just a bit.

With a few more determined twists, the ropes loosen enough for me to pull one hand free.

"Yes!" I whisper triumphantly to myself. My fingers are numb, but I quickly work on freeing my other hand. Once I'm completely untied, I rub my sore wrists, trying to bring back some feeling into them.

I stand up, my legs shaky but functional. I start searching the room, looking for any sort of window or hidden door.

My search reveals a small, grimy window high up on the wall. It's not ideal, but it's something. I drag the chair over, wincing at the screeching noise it makes against the floor. Standing on the chair, I reach the window and push against it. It's stuck, but I'm not giving up. I push harder, throwing my weight into it, and finally, it creaks open.

Cool air hits my face and I take a deep breath, feeling a renewed sense of hope. The window is small, but I'm determined. I start to squeeze through, the rough edges scraping against my skin. It's a tight fit, but inch by inch, I manage to get myself through the opening.

I drop quietly from the window and find myself in a narrow, dimly lit hallway. I'm free from the room, but not out of danger yet. I need to be smart and move quickly as possible.

I tiptoe down the hallway, every sense heightened. I have no idea where I am, but I need to find an exit, a phone, something to help me get back to Ivan.

I turn a corner and freeze. Another hallway, longer than the previous one, doors lining each side. It's eerily quiet, the kind of quiet that screams hidden danger. My mind races, urging me to make a decision. Forward or back?

HIS DEMANDS | 235

Before I can choose, a door swings open ahead of me. My heart sinks as Boris steps out, flanked by two of his men.

His face twists into a cruel smile. "You don't give up do you?" he taunts.

I back away, but it's pointless. The men grab me, their grips iron-tight. Boris' eyes are cold and menacing.

"Seems you need a lesson in staying put," he says, his voice unnervingly calm.

Every nerve-ending fires within, signaling a fight-or-flight response at the terror of not knowing what's to come.

CHAPTER 37

IVAN

Fyodor and I move stealthily yet quickly toward the back of the run-down strip club. Every second counts with Julie's life hanging in the balance.

As we round the corner, I spot a guard stationed at the back door. His stance is relaxed, unaware of the storm about to hit him. In a split second my years of training kick in, honing my focus to a razor's edge.

I charge without a moment's hesitation. The guard barely has time to register my approach before I'm on him. My first strike is a swift upward palm to his nose, stunning him. As he reels, I follow up with a sharp elbow to his throat, cutting off his air and any chance of a shout for help. His hands claw at his neck, panic setting in.

I don't let up. Spinning behind him, I lock my arm around his neck in a chokehold. He thrashes, but my grip is vice-like. With a calculated squeeze, his struggles weaken, his body going limp in my arms. I lower him to the ground, ensuring he's out cold.

Fyodor, having watched the takedown, whistles lowly. "Impressive, Ivan. Remind me never to get on your bad side."

I smirk as I wipe my hands on my pants, a mix of adrenaline and satisfaction coursing through me. "Just doing what's necessary."

We cautiously approach the back door. My heart pounds fiercely in my chest, not just from the exertion but from the fear of what we might find inside. Julie's in there somewhere, and every instinct I have screams to get to her fast, that she's in imminent danger.

I try the door—locked. No surprise there. I glance at Fyodor, who nods, understanding the unspoken plan. We need to be swift and silent. The element of surprise is all we have.

I pull out a small toolkit from my jacket pocket, old habits die hard I guess. In seconds, I have the lock picked, the door easing open with a soft creak. We slip inside, the darkness of the club swallowing us whole.

The place reeks of cheap perfume and stale beer, the air heavy with the scent of despair. We stand still for a moment, allowing our eyes to adjust to the difference in light, or lack thereof. The silence is oppressive, and I strain my ears for any sound, any hint of where they might be holding Julie.

The back rooms of the strip club are a labyrinth of decay and neglect. As Fyodor and I move cautiously through the dimly lit corridors, the air is thick with the stench of mold and rot. The once vibrant wallpaper is peeling off, revealing patches of water-stained walls beneath. The carpet under our feet is sticky and stained, a mute testament to the countless spills and uncleanliness of the place.

Every room we pass is a snapshot of desolation—empty stages with torn curtains, chairs scattered haphazardly, and tables coated with a film of dust. The atmosphere is heavy with the ghosts of revelry long past. It's a place that reeks of hopelessness, a far cry from the glitz and glamor one might expect from a club.

I grip my weapon tighter, ready for whatever might come.

Suddenly, I hear voices. My senses heighten, every nerve on edge. I signal to Fyodor, and we inch closer to the source. The muffled sounds of laughter and clinking glasses reach us. Peeking through a slightly ajar door, I see a room that looks like a private lounge, its once luxurious fittings now faded and frayed.

Three men lounge on sofas, bottles of beer in hand, their laughter echoing grotesquely in the dingy room. They're engrossed in their conversation, oblivious to the world outside their drunken bubble. My eyes scan the room, searching, until they land on a figure slumped on a couch.

It's Julie.

My heart lurches at the sight. She's handcuffed, her head lolling to one side, a trickle of blood marring her forehead. Anger boils within me, a seething, raw fury at the sight of her, so vulnerable and defenseless.

I take a deep breath, forcing myself to stay calm and think clearly. Charging in recklessly won't help her. We need a plan, and fast.

Fyodor meets my gaze, his eyes reflecting my own rage. He understands the stakes without a word being spoken. We've shared a silent understanding since we were kids, a tight bond between brothers. We retreat from the door, moving back into the shadows to strategize.

"We need to take them out quietly," I whisper, my voice a harsh rasp. "We can't risk them hurting Julie any more than they already have."

Fyodor nods, pulling out a small knife. "I'll take the one on the left. You got the other two?"

I nod, my hand tightening around my weapon. "On my signal."

We edge back to the door, our movements synchronized. The men inside continue their carousing, unaware of our approach. My eyes are fixed on Julie.

Before I can act, Fyodor's firm grip on my arm pulls me back. He nods toward the doorway behind us, a flicker of urgency flashing in his eyes.

I turn to see five men silently filing into the room, each one exuding an air of professional calm. The FBI has arrived, just in time.

I quickly point out Julie to the agents. One of them, a tall man with a stern face, nods in acknowledgment and signals to his team.

The raid erupts into chaos in a barrage of gunfire, shattering the oppressive silence of the rundown club. The FBI agents, their movements a blend of precision and deadly grace, dive into action, returning fire while seeking cover behind the dilapidated furnishings.

I'm momentarily frozen, the cacophony of gunshots echoing through the grimy, neon-lit space jolting every nerve in my body. Fyodor's face is a mask of concentration as he grabs my arm, his grip tight. "Ivan, stay back!" he shouts over the sound of gunfire.

But my eyes are fixed on Julie, slumped and vulnerable on that filthy couch. The sight ignites a fire within me, a primal urge that overpowers reason. I wrench my arm free from Fyodor's grasp and lunge forward, staying low to avoid the flying bullets.

The agents are a whirlwind of controlled violence, systematically taking down Boris' men. But in the midst of the disorder, Boris spots my reckless charge. His eyes, cold and calculating, lock onto Julie.

With a swift, predatory movement, he seizes her limp form, dragging her up as a human shield. His retreat is methodical, the chaotic firefight a distraction that allows him to move toward the back exit. Julie's head lolls helplessly as he maneuvers her in front of him, her life hanging by a thread in his ruthless grasp.

Rage—raw and unbridled—courses through me. Every instinct screams to charge forward, to tear Boris away from her and ensure her safety. But I know that a direct assault would put Julie at even greater risk.

Fyodor yells something, but his words are lost in the roar of gunfire. My focus narrows to Boris and Julie, the rest of the world fading into a blur. I move with a singular purpose, weaving through the mayhem, every sense attuned to their retreating figures.

Boris reaches the back door, his grip on Julie unyielding. He glances back, his eyes meeting mine for a fleeting moment, an evil smirk playing on his lips. It's a look of triumph, of knowing he's once again manipulated the situation to his advantage.

He drags Julie toward the van, his intentions clear; he going to throw her in the back and disappear into the labyrinth of the city. But the FBI agents—along with Fyodor and myself—close in around him, a tightening net of law and unbridled fury on my part.

I step forward, my voice calm yet firm, trying to reason with the cornered predator. "Boris, there's nowhere to go," I call out, hoping to pierce the bubble of his desperation. "You're surrounded. Let her go!"

Boris' back is to the van, Julie held tight in his grasp. She begins to come to, her face a mask of pain, confusion, and fear. His hand is shaking as he presses the gun to her temple, his eyes wild and unpredictable. "Back off!" he shouts, the gun trembling against Julie's skin. "Unless you want her dead, you'll let me leave with her!"

The agents hold their fire, in position with their weapons raised but hesitant to risk Julie's life. Fyodor is standing beside me with clenched fists, a silent fury in his eyes, a thick vein twitching in his temple.

The agents stand their ground, guns trained on Boris, but no one dares to make a move that might provoke him to pull the trigger. Fyodor glances at me, waiting for my cue.

I raise my hands, a gesture of false surrender, my gaze locked on him. "Boris, there's nowhere to go," I say, my voice calm but laced with a silent promise of retribution. "Let her go, and you might have a chance."

Julie's face is pale and streaked with blood, and she's barely conscious. But beneath her dazed exterior, a spark of defiance flickers. In a sudden burst of energy, she frees one arm and drives her elbow hard into Boris' gut before twirling herself away from his body.

The unexpected blow catches Boris off guard, causing his grip on Julie and the gun to falter. It's the opportunity I've been waiting for. In one fluid, practiced motion, I draw my gun and fire. The bullet finds its mark, hitting Boris squarely between the eyes.

He crumples to the ground, his life extinguished in an instant. The agents rush forward but my focus is solely on Julie. As Boris' dead hand releases her, I catch her just before she hits the ground.

"Julie!" I call out, cradling her in my arms. Her eyes flutter closed, her body finally succumbing to the strain and trauma of the ordeal. My heart pounds in my chest, fear and relief battling for dominance.

Fyodor is by my side in an instant, his face etched with concern. "Is she okay?"

I gently brush the hair from her face, examining her for any further injuries. "She's unconscious," I say.

The agents move about the area, their movements efficient and methodical. One of them is on the phone, requesting paramedics and multiple ambulances.

I hold Julie gently to my chest, unsure of the extent of her wounds. The woman I love is unconscious in my arms, having just endured hours of terror with a madman. I make a silent vow that I will never again allow any harm to come to her. I will do whatever it takes to build a life of safety, one free from the shadows of my past.

CHAPTER 38

IVAN

I grip Julie's hand tightly as the ambulance races into the night. The paramedics had quickly assessed her condition, determining that she likely had a concussion. Her consciousness came and went, her words slurred and disjointed as she fought to stay awake.

I couldn't bear to be separated from her so I insisted on riding in the ambulance, kneeling beside her stretcher. The paramedic riding in the back worked around us, attaching monitors and administering oxygen. Every so often, Julie would push the mask off her face, her eyes searching for mine, her grip on my hand tightening.

In one of her more lucid moments after pulling the mask down, she gripped my hand tightly in hers. Her voice was urgent, a startling clarity in her eyes as she said, "Ivan, tell the doctor I'm pregnant." The words hit me like a physical blow, a revelation that sent my heart into overdrive.

"Pregnant?" I echoed, my voice barely more than a whisper. A surge of emotions flooded through me all at once—joy, fear, surprise. "Julie, how long have you known?"

Before she can answer her eyes flutter, and she slips back into unconsciousness. The paramedic quickly replaces the mask over her face.

I sit there, stunned, my mind whirling. *Pregnant.* We're going to have a baby. The joy of the news battles with the uncertainty of Julie's condition and the horror of what just occurred.

I hold her hand, watching her every breath, every slight movement. The paramedics reassure me that they are doing everything they can, but the ride to the hospital feels like an eternity.

As the ambulance speeds through the streets of New York, the city lights blur past us in a stream of colors. I keep whispering to her, telling her to hold on, that everything is going to be okay, that our baby needs her, that *I* need her.

My mind races with plans and promises, a future that suddenly seems both bright and frighteningly uncertain. The weight of responsibility, the need to protect and provide for my family, feels both overwhelming and invigorating.

The ambulance finally screeches to a halt at the hospital, and the paramedics quickly wheel Julie in. I follow close behind, my heart in my throat, conjuring the courage to be able to deal with whatever comes next. As we rush into the ER, I make a silent vow to Julie and our unborn child that I will do whatever it takes to keep them safe, to give them the life they deserve.

Under the fluorescent lights of the hospital waiting room, I pace back and forth, each step marking my mounting anxiety and restless thoughts. The antiseptic smell of the hospital mingles with the scent of fear and uncertainty that seems to permeate the air. My mind is a whirlwind of regret and worry, replaying the events that led us here, each moment a sharp stab of self-reproach.

I keep seeing Julie's face, the way she looked at me in the ambulance, the urgency in her voice when she revealed her pregnancy. My heart clenches at the memory, weighed down by a heavy mix of love and guilt. I should have told her I loved her then and there, should have expressed the depth of my feelings when I had the chance. But the words remained unspoken, trapped within me.

I force myself to breathe, to remain calm, but a gnawing fear for our unborn child tugs at my consciousness. The day's trauma, the violence and stress, will our baby be able to survive it? The thought causes a sharp pang in my chest, hope and dread battling within me.

I resume my pacing, my footsteps a rhythmic reminder of the helplessness I feel. The waiting is agonizing, each second stretching into an eternity. I want to be with her, to hold her hand, to be there when she wakes up. But all I can do is wait, trapped in a limbo of uncertainty.

The doctors had been guarded in their responses, their professional demeanor doing little to ease my worries. They spoke of monitoring her concussion and vitals of the need to assess any potential complications with the pregnancy. Their words were clinical, but the underlying message was clear—the next few hours would be critical.

HIS DEMANDS | 247

As I continue my anxious pacing, the door to the waiting room opens, immediately drawing my attention. Fyodor walks in, his expression grim, accompanied by Barb. She looks disheveled, her usual sharp appearance clouded by distress and anger. The sight of her in such a state deepens the knot of worry in my stomach.

"Barb, what happened?" I ask, my voice tinged with concern as I approach them.

She shakes her head, her eyes blazing with a mix of fury and pain. "I got home just as they were loading that bastard Calvin into the ambulance," she spits out, her voice trembling with rage. "He told me what he did, the lowlife. If I'd had a gun, I swear I would've shot him again myself."

Fyodor places a comforting hand on her shoulder, but she seems too consumed by her emotions to notice. "He set Julie up, Ivan. Lured her out with a lie about me being hurt. And now..." Her voice cracks, revealing the fear beneath her anger.

I feel a surge of protectiveness, both for Julie and Barb. "I'm sorry, Barb. This is all my fault. If I hadn't—"

Barb cuts me off, her eyes locking onto mine. "Don't you dare start with that 'it's all my fault' crap, Ivan. We both know who's to blame here, and it's not you nor is it me." Her fierceness is a testament to her strength, even in the face of such betrayal and turmoil.

Fyodor interjects, trying to diffuse the tension. "We're all on edge right now. The important thing is that Julie is safe, and we're going to make sure she stays that way."

Barb nods. "You're damn right we will. And as for Calvin..." She trails off, her gaze hardening. "Let's just say he's going to regret the day he ever crossed paths with me."

I look between them, grateful for their support but weighed down by the enormity of the situation. I sit down in one of the chairs. "I should've seen this coming," I admit, my guilt resurfacing. "I thought I'd left that world behind, but it came back to haunt us all."

"We'll deal with it, Ivan. Together," Fyodor says, his voice steady. "Right now, our focus is on Julie and the baby. We'll handle whatever comes after."

Barb nods in agreement, her earlier rage giving way to a new focus. "We're here for you, Ivan. For Julie. Whatever it takes, we'll get through this."

Their words are a small comfort in the sea of uncertainty that surrounds us. I nod, feeling a renewed sense of purpose. "Thank you, both of you. Right now, all I can do is wait and hope that Julie and our child are going to be okay."

In the midst of my guilt-ridden thoughts, the doctor emerges, drawing all of our attention. He looks around the room, his eyes settling on me.

"Mr. Stepanov?" he asks, his tone professional yet empathetic.

I stand up immediately, my heart racing. "Yes, that's me. How is she? How's Julie?"

The doctor offers a small, reassuring smile. "She's stable. She's been asking for you. Would you like to see her?" It's a foolish question.

Relief washes over me, mingled with lingering concern. "Yes, absolutely. But how is she really? And the baby?"

He hesitates for a moment, choosing his words carefully. "She's suffered a severe concussion due to multiple blows to her head, but she's conscious and responsive. As for the pregnancy, it's still early, but we're monitoring her closely."

I nod, my mind racing with a mix of relief and worry not to mention an even greater hatred toward Boris for hurting her. "Can I go in now?"

"Yes, of course," the doctor replies, gesturing toward the corridor.

I turn to Barb and Fyodor, anxious expressions on their faces. "I'll let you know how she's doing as soon as I can," I promise them.

Barb nods, her expression softening. "Tell her we're here for her, Ivan."

"And if there's anything she needs, anything at all, you let us know," Fyodor adds.

I give them a grateful nod, feeling the sincerity of their support. "I will. Thank you both."

With a deep breath, I follow the doctor down the hallway, every fiber of my being aching to see Julie. I enter the room to find Julie lying there, a bandage wrapped around her head, but her eyes are open, and there's a smile on her face. It's a sight that both relieves and pains me.

"Julie," I breathe out, rushing to her side, taking her hands in mine. I can barely contain the emotions surging through me.

She tries to speak but I interrupt her, my words tumbling out in a rush of apology. "I'm so sorry, Julie. I never should have put you in this situation. I—"

But she cuts me off, her voice weak but filled with warmth. "Ivan, it's okay. I'm okay."

I shake my head, unable to accept her forgiveness so easily. "No, it's not okay. I should have protected you better. I..."

She squeezes my hands, her eyes shining with unshed tears, a mix of joy and relief. "Ivan, I need to tell you something."

My heart beats faster, a mixture of anticipation and concern. "What is it? Is everything okay?"

Her smile returns, brighter than before, as if a weight has been lifted off her shoulders. "It's more than okay. When they did the ultrasound to check the baby's heartbeat, they found something. Two somethings actually."

I stare at her, dumbfounded for a minute, causing her to laugh. "Two heartbeats. We're having twins."

The revelation hits me with the force of a thunderbolt, joy and astonishment flooding through me. Twins. Two little lives growing inside her, a doubling of the miracle we'd already been blessed with.

I lean in closer, my heart swelling with a love and excitement I've never known before. "Twins... Julie, that's incredible." I'm at a loss for words, the news rendering me speechless with happiness.

She nods, her tears now flowing freely, mirroring my own. "Yes, twins. Our family is growing, Ivan. We're going to have two beautiful babies."

In that moment, with the revelation that we're having twins hanging in the air between us, I realize just how much my life has changed, how much she has changed me. From a solitary existence to a life bursting with love and the promise of new beginnings; Julie, my wife, my love, and now the mother of our twins.

What more could a man want?

EPILOGUE I

JULIE

Almost seven months later...

Sitting across from Barb at a cozy lunch spot, I can't help but chuckle at her exaggerated eye roll. "I told you, Julie, stop reading those articles. They're just going to freak you out more," she says, sipping her tea.

I rest a hand on my significantly rounded belly, feeling a little kick from one of the twins. "I know, I know," I reply, trying to find a comfortable position in my chair for the hundredth time. "But it's hard not to worry. Especially with two of them in there."

Barb shakes her head, smiling. "You're doing great, sweetie. You've only got three weeks left. You're almost at the finish line."

I nod, taking a bite of my salad. "It's just... everything feels so real now. It's not just me anymore; it's these two little lives as well." I pause, feeling another kick, stronger this time. "They're quite the soccer players already."

Barb laughs, her eyes twinkling with affection. "They're going to keep you on your toes, that's for sure."

Barb's expression turns more serious and the conversation shifts. "How have you been doing, really? I know it's been a while, but still. That was serious trauma you went through."

I meet her gaze, appreciating her concern. "Honestly, I'm okay. It was terrifying, and there were moments I wasn't sure I'd make it out. But I did. And I think it's made me stronger." I pause, my hand instinctively moving to my belly again. "I had to be strong, for them."

Barb reaches across the table, covering my hand with hers. "You're one of the toughest people I know. I'm just glad you're safe, and these little ones, too."

Barb smiles but a concerned expression still shadows her face. "And your father? Please tell me he's staying away from you."

I pause for a moment, the memory of my father's betrayal still raw. "He's recovered from the gunshot wound, as far as I know," I say, trying to keep my tone neutral. "But thankfully, he hasn't tried to contact me since. I hope he finally gets it that he needs to stay out of my life for good, that he cannot be a part of it.

Barb reaches across the table again, giving my hand a reassuring squeeze. "I'm glad he's leaving you alone. You don't need that kind of drama in your life, especially with two little ones on the way."

I smile, feeling a warmth spread through me. It's not just the pregnancy glow; it's the love and support I've received from the people closest to me, especially Barb. She's been a rock through all the ups and downs.

"I couldn't have done it without you, Aunt Barb. You've been there for me through everything. I don't know what I'd do without you," I say, my voice thick with emotion.

Barb gives my hand another gentle squeeze. "You're family, Julie. And family sticks together, no matter what. Now, let's talk about something happier. Have you and Ivan decided on names yet?"

I laugh, glad for the change in topic. "Oh, you know Ivan. He's got a list of names a mile long. I think we're down to the final ten though."

Barb raises an eyebrow. "Only ten? You're going to have to start making some decisions soon, mama."

I nod, my heart full of excitement and love for the lives growing inside me, and the future that awaits us. "We will. This is going to be one hell of an adventure."

Waddling back to the office, I can't help but smile at the beautiful Manhattan day unfolding around me. Ivan always insists on having the driver take me everywhere, but I'm stubborn, always have been. I enjoy these short walks, the independence they offer, and let's be honest, at this point, I need all the exercise I can get.

The city is bustling, the sounds and sights a familiar comfort. People rush past, absorbed in their own worlds, and I feel a sense of contentment as I take my time, moving at my own pace. The sun is warm on my face, a gentle breeze plays with my hair, and I feel so grateful for this moment.

As I slowly make my way, I think about everything that's happened. The kidnapping seems like a lifetime ago, a dark chapter that's been closed, allowing Ivan and me to focus on the brighter future ahead. I rub my belly, smiling at the thought of meeting our twins. Life is going to change dramatically, but I'm ready for it—more than ready.

I think about Ivan, how much he's changed since we first met. He's more open, more vulnerable, and in turn, our relationship has deepened in ways I never expected. He's going to be an amazing father, and I can't wait to see him with our twins.

I pass by a small park and watch the children play, their laughter ringing through the air. It's a sound I'm looking forward to hearing in my own home soon. I imagine Ivan and me taking our twins here, pushing them on the swings, watching them explore the world with wide, curious eyes.

My phone buzzes in my bag, and I pull it out to see a message from Ivan. It's a simple *I love you*, but it brings a wide smile to my face. I quickly type back a response, telling him I love him too, and that I'm on my way back to the office.

I continue to take in the hustle and bustle of the city, feeling a profound sense of belonging. This city, with all its chaos and beauty, is where I've found love, where I've built my life, and where I'm about to start my family.

I reach the office building, a little out of breath but feeling good. The doorman greets me with a friendly smile, and I return it, feeling a surge of happiness.

Stepping into the Goodacre Cares office, nestled on the fourth floor of Ivan's building, I can't help but feel a sense of pride. It's still a small operation—just me and a few dedicated employees—but it's mine, and it's making a difference.

As I waddle through the office, I'm greeted by the familiar faces of my team. There's Shannon, our outreach coordinator, always buzzing with energy and ideas. "Morning, Julie! The new pamphlets came in. They look fantastic!" she exclaims, waving a colorful brochure at me.

"That's great, Shannon! Let's make sure they get distributed to all the local shelters by the end of the week," I reply, thrilled at the progress we're making.

Then there's Alex, the quiet but brilliant finance guy who's been a godsend for keeping our accounts and grants in order. "Hey, Julie, did you see the email about the grant approval? We got it!" he says, a rare smile spreading across his face.

I clap my hands together in excitement. "That's amazing news! That grant will help fund our next workshop series. Great work on that application!"

As I continue toward my office, I pass by Mia, our volunteer coordinator, who's deep in conversation on the phone. She gives me a thumbs up, signaling that the volunteer training session is all set.

Finally reaching my office, I settle into my chair with a little effort, courtesy of my expanding belly. I gaze out the window at the sprawling city below, my hand resting on my stomach, feeling the gentle kicks of our twins. It's moments like these that I take a second to reflect on how far I've come.

Starting Goodacre Cares has been a dream come true. It's my way of giving back, of using my experiences to help others find their way out of darkness. And with each day, each small victory, I feel like we're making a real difference.

I smile, a deep sense of contentment washing over me. Despite everything we've been through, the challenges and the fears, I know this is where I'm meant to be. Building a better future, not just for myself and my family, but for all those who come through the doors of Goodacre Cares, seeking help and hope.

With a deep breath, I turn back to my desk, ready to dive into the day's work. There's a stack of papers in my inbox filled with future marketing ideas and potential workshops as well as plenty of emails to respond to. The work never stops, but neither does the passion and drive that fuels it.

Settling into my office chair, I'm ready to dive into the afternoon workload. Just as I open my laptop, a sudden sensation stops me in my tracks. It's subtle at first, a mere whisper of discomfort. But then it comes again, unmistakable this time. My water has broken. My heart leaps with a mix of excitement and nerves. This is it. It's happening. The twins are coming.

Trying to stay calm, I pick up my phone and text Ivan.

Hey, it's time.

Ivan's reaction is instant. In what feels like mere seconds, he bursts into my office, his face a picture of excitement and concern. "We need to get you to the hospital," he says, pulling me to my feet.

"Ivan! Slow down," I protest playfully, even though I secretly love his protective nature.

He rushes me to the elevator, practically vibrating with excitement, his eyes shining with the thrill of the moment. But beneath that excitement, I can sense his worry. "They're a bit early," he murmurs, more to himself than to me.

I squeeze his hand reassuringly. "Remember the doctor said twins usually do come early. And it's only three weeks," I say, smiling through another contraction.

He looks at me, a mixture of awe and love in his eyes. "You're incredible," he says, his voice filled with emotion.

After we get into the elevator, I lean against Ivan, drawing comfort from his presence. This is a moment we've been waiting for, the beginning of a new chapter in our lives. The journey hasn't been easy, but here we are, together, about to welcome our twins into the world.

The contraction passes, and I take a deep breath, bracing myself for the next one. Ivan holds me close, his warmth and strength a constant reassurance. I can't help but think about how much our lives are about to change, how these two little beings are going to bring so much joy along with chaos into our world.

As the elevator glides upward, a sense of confusion washes over me. "Ivan, aren't we going to the hospital? Why are we going up?" I ask, my brows furrowing in puzzlement.

Ivan's eyes twinkle with that sly, mischievous look I've come to adore. "You really think I'm going to let you sit through Manhattan traffic while you're in labor?" he says, his voice filled with a mix of humor and seriousness.

I'm about to protest but my words are cut off as the elevator doors slide open, revealing the rooftop. My eyes widen in shock and disbelief. There, right in front of us, is a private helicopter, its blades slowly spinning, ready for takeoff.

Ivan helps me out of the elevator, a proud smile playing on his lips. "I've had this helicopter on standby for the past couple of weeks, just in case," he explains, his voice filled with eagerness.

I can't help but laugh, a sound that's half disbelief, half sheer joy. "You're insane," I say, still giggling. "This is so incredibly over the top."

He grins back at me as he helps me into the helicopter. "Maybe so, but I want the best for you and our babies. Plus, I couldn't resist making a grand entrance to parenthood."

The pilot greets us warmly, and within moments, we're strapped in and lifting into the sky. The city spreads out below us, a vast tapestry of buildings and streets, shrinking as we rise higher and higher.

Looking out the window, I'm struck by the beauty of the city from this vantage point. It's a view I've never seen before, and it takes my breath away. The contractions are coming stronger now, but the excitement of the moment makes them more bearable.

Ivan takes my hand, squeezing it gently. "You're doing great," he says as I concentrate on my breathing, his voice reassuring. "We'll be at the hospital in no time."

I turn to him, my heart swelling with love. "This is so crazy. You and your surprises," I say, my voice soft with affection.

He leans over and kisses me, a gentle, loving kiss that speaks volumes. "I'll always do whatever it takes for you and our children," he whispers against my lips. "You're my world, Julie."

As we fly over the city, heading toward the hospital, I lean back in my seat. Oddly, I am feeling a sense of peace and contentment, despite the fact that I am in labor about to give birth to twins. Ivan's love and dedication are evident in every action he takes, every word he speaks. I know, without a doubt, that he'll be an incredible father, just as he's been an incredible husband.

EPILOGUE II

IVAN

Two years later...

In the sanctum of my home office, I'm immersed in the intricacies of my latest business project. The grandeur of our new mansion, located just outside the city, offers a peaceful retreat from the bustling energy of Manhattan. It's a spacious, luxurious haven where we can unwind and enjoy family time.

My concentration on the spreadsheet in front of me falters as the delightful sound of tiny feet pattering against the hardwood floors drifts into the room. The giggles and squeals of our twin girls, now two years old, fill the house with a lively energy that's impossible to ignore.

I lean back in my chair, allowing myself a moment to bask in the joyful commotion that has become our life. The sound of Julie's voice, a mix of laughter and gentle admonishments, echoes through the halls as she chases after our little ones. Her attempts to wrangle the twins into some semblance of order are met with playful resistance, their tiny voices bubbling with laughter and mischief.

I can't help but smile, a deep feeling of contentment washing over me. These moments, these simple pleasures of family life, are what I cherish the most. The sound of their laughter and the warmth of their presence is such a stark contrast to the solitude and cold apathy that once defined my life.

Pushing away from my desk, I decide that work can wait. These moments are fleeting, and I don't want to miss a single one. I step out of my office and into the hallway, following the sounds of giggles and play.

As I round the corner, I see them. Julie, her hair a little disheveled, has a look of mock exasperation on her face, our daughters in tow. The girls are a whirlwind of energy, their bright eyes sparkling with delight as they spot me.

"Daddy!" they both squeal in unison, their tiny arms outstretched as they run toward me. I scoop them up, one in each arm, their laughter infectious.

Julie walks over, her eyes shining with love and a touch of fatigue. "Your turn," she says with a playful smirk. "I'm starting to think they have more energy than both of us combined."

I kiss her forehead, a gesture of affection and gratitude. "I wouldn't have it any other way," I say, the girls giggling as they cling to me.

As we head toward the living room, our steps light and carefree, I reflect on how much my life has changed. The man who once lived only for business and power now finds his greatest joy in the laughter of his children and in the love of his wife.

Our family, our home, it's a world I never imagined myself in, a world that's more fulfilling than any business deal or corporate success. In the eyes of my daughters and the smile of my wife, I've found a happiness that's profound and real.

We settle into the living room, the girls showing off their latest drawings, their voices a melody of excitement and pride. Julie and I exchange a look, a silent understanding of the beautiful life we've built together.

As the sun begins its descent, painting the sky in hues of orange and pink, I glance at Julie, her eyes weary yet filled with the unmistakable glow of motherhood. "You've done enough for today," I say with a smile, my voice laced with affection. Leaning in, I plant a gentle kiss on her forehead, a silent token of my appreciation and love.

Hoisting our twin girls higher into my arms, their giggles and wiggles a lively symphony, I head toward the staircase. Elizabeth clings to my neck, her laughter a melody that fills the hall, while Ana playfully tugs at my hair, her mischievous grin infectious. As we ascend the stairs, their excitement is palpable, their energy boundless.

The bath time ritual is nothing short of an adventure. Splashes and bubbles fill the air as I gently bathe each of them. Elizabeth, ever the imaginative one, conjures up tales of mermaids and underwater castles, her tiny hands mimicking the waves. Ana, with her boundless energy, splashes with gusto, her laughter ringing through the bathroom.

By the time they're both clean, dried, and snug in their pajamas, I find myself thoroughly soaked, my shirt clinging to my skin. But the sight of their rosy cheeks and eyes bright full of love and trust, makes every drop of water worth it. I can't help but laugh along with them, their joy infectious, their spirits unbridled.

As I carry them to their room, my thoughts drift to the journey that brought me here. Fatherhood was a role I never anticipated, a chapter in my life I hadn't dared to imagine. It was something I wanted but never expected. But now, holding my daughters close, feeling their warmth against me, I realize how much they've transformed me.

Each giggle, each hug, each wide-eyed wonder at the world around them, adds a richness to my life I never knew was missing. They are my heart walking outside my body, a love so profound and all-consuming that it reshapes my very being.

I look at them, their faces a perfect blend of Julie and me, and I'm struck by the miracle of their existence. These little girls, with their mother's grace and my determination, have become the center of my universe. Their laughter is my greatest joy, their happiness my ultimate goal.

I tuck them into bed, their tiny hands wrapped around my fingers, their eyelids fluttering closed. In this quiet moment, I reflect on the life Julie and I have built together. A life that once felt incomplete is now brimming with love, laughter, and the sweetness of family.

As I softly close the door to the girls' bedroom, their gentle breathing a lullaby of peace, I call out to Julie. There's no response, but it doesn't concern me. Our home, vast and sprawling, often feels like a small world of its own, where one can easily slip into a quiet corner, lost in thought or work.

With a contented sigh, I make my way to the master bedroom, my mind still replaying the joyful chaos of bath time. The girls' laughter echoes in my memory, a reminder of the simple pleasures that now define my life.

I pour myself a glass of whiskey, the rich, amber liquid swirling in the glass, a perfect end to a day filled with family joys. The smooth warmth of the drink is a familiar comfort, a moment of solitude in the midst of our bustling household.

Stepping into our bedroom I expect the usual quiet, the soft glow of the bedside lamp casting a serene ambiance. But what greets me is a sight that brings an immediate smile to my face, a pleasant surprise that quickens my pulse.

Julie, radiant and alluring, reclines on the bed, adorned in lingerie that accentuates her beauty in ways that words can't capture. The sight of her, so confident and inviting, ignites a fire within me, a reminder of the passion that simmers just beneath the surface of our daily routines.

"What's the occasion?" I ask, the tone of my voice a mix of amusement and desire as I approach her.

She looks up at me, her eyes sparkling with a playful mischief. "Well, I was thinking," she begins, her voice sultry and teasing. "It's about time we started working on another set of twins, don't you think?"

The suggestion, so boldly and enticingly presented, sends a thrill through me. The idea of expanding our family, of experiencing once again the miracle of life with Julie, fills me with a profound excitement.

I set my glass aside, my focus entirely on her.

"I couldn't agree more."

Like a wild animal, I pounce.

The moment I'm on the bed with her, Julie's hands are on my body, deft and sure, and her touch is electric. I'm enraptured by her, lost in the moment and the promise of what's to come. She draws me into a deep, passionate kiss, and I melt into her, eager and ready. She undoes the buttons of my shirt, exposing my bare chest.

"God, you're beautiful," I say, taking in the sight of her gorgeous body clad in nothing but her flirty lingerie. "How the hell did I ever resist you for so long?"

As Julie's hands explore my body, I find myself swept away by the sensation, the intimate connection we share. I reach around, opening the clasp of her bra and letting her full breasts tumble out. Her body, already as sublime as they come, has only grown more beautiful since motherhood. There's a glow to her, cliché as it may sound, that makes her irresistible. She soon has me naked, her in nothing but her lacy panties.

Her touch, as always, is intoxicating. Her lips are soft, her skin is smooth, and her body is warm against mine. She smells of vanilla and spice, and her touch leaves trails of heat and tingling sensations in its wake. I can't get enough of her, and she seems equally eager to please. She knows exactly how to touch me, where to kiss me, how to drive me wild with desire.

Julie takes hold of my cock, stroking it slowly, my own hand finding the liquid warmth between her thighs. She closes her eyes and sighs as she strokes me, her heavy breasts rising and falling as I tease her clit, coaxing her closer and closer to orgasm.

"Come for me, my love," I say. "Now."

She smiles and nods, and just like that an orgasm rushes through her. She sighs and moans, bucking hard against my touch. Her gorgeous eyes open wide when the pleasure fades.

"I need you," she says. "Don't make me wait another moment."

"Have I told you how much I love how bossy you can be?"

She laughs, but there's not a chance I can resist her any longer. I peel off her thong panties and toss them aside, her pussy glistening with arousal. I move over top of her, Julie looking up at me with those eyes that I've found myself lost in so many times.

Love is interesting in how it deepens over time, how it becomes richer, more complex, with every day that passes, every moment you share with your beloved. Even in tender moments such as these, I find myself overwhelmed with excitement for what's yet to come for the two of us, how much we have to share, to experience together.

But just as important is staying in the here and now, never losing sight of how wonderful each individual moment can be. I glide into her, Julie's womanhood gripping me with that perfect sensation, her softness surrounding me. I push into her slowly at first, her hands settling on my rear and taking hold.

We're both lost in the moment, caught up in the heat of passion. Her hands are everywhere, her lips following close behind. We're moving together now, our bodies in perfect sync, sharing a pleasure so intense it's almost unbearable. It's an ecstasy unlike anything I've ever known, and I never want it to end.

Soon we're climaxing together, my seed spilling into her, Julie's perfect face tight with total, unbridled ecstasy. I hold her, kiss her, caress her as we lay wrapped in one another's arms, gazing into each other's eyes.

"I love you, Ivan."

"And I love you."

We continue to kiss and all I can think about is the happiness I feel knowing there are so many more nights like this to come.

How did one man deserve so much luck?

The End

Printed in Dunstable, United Kingdom